W9-AEN-622

Marsh & Me

Also by Martine Murray

Molly & Pim and the Millions of Stars

Marsh & Me

Martine Murray

Alfred A. Knopf
New York

THIS IS A BORZOI BOOK PUBLISHED BY ALFRED A. KNOPF

All rights reserved. Published in the United States by Alfred A. Knopf, an imprint of Random House Children's Books, a division of Penguin Random House LLC, New York. Originally published in slightly different form in paperback in Australia by Text Publishing, Melbourne, Australia, in 2017.

Knopf, Borzoi Books, and the colophon are registered trademarks of Penguin Random House LLC.

Visit us on the Web! rhcbooks.com

Educators and librarians, for a variety of teaching tools, visit us at RHTeachersLibrarians.com

Library of Congress Cataloging-in-Publication Data
Name: Murray, Martine, author.
Title: Marsh and me / Martine Murray.
Description: First American edition. | New York : Alfred A. Knopf, [2019] |
Summary: When Joey, a loner whose life consists of home, school, and the hill where he plays guitar, meets Marsh, she opens his eyes to a new world.
Identifiers: LCCN 2017055717 | ISBN 978-0-399-55044-7 (trade) |
ISBN 978-0-399-55045-4 (lib. bdg.) | ISBN 978-0-399-55046-1 (ebook)
Subjects: | CYAC: Friendship—Fiction. | Self-confidence—Fiction. |
Guitar—Fiction. | Family life—Fiction. | Serbian Americans—Fiction. |
Grief—Fiction. | Single-parent families—Fiction.
Classification: LCC PZ7.M9637 Feb 2019 | DDC [Fic]—dc23

The text of this book is set in 12-point Calisto MT Pro.

Printed in the United States of America
February 2019
10 9 8 7 6 5 4 3 2 1

First American Edition

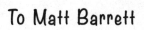

To Matt Barrett

From all the little things, she rose.

—Jelena Dinic

The Hill

There are three places in my life. Hill, home and school. If you drew a map of me, I would be triangular. Or if you drew a portrait of me, I would have three aspects. Maybe even three heads. I'd like a painting of a three-headed me, but that's because I suspect I'm secretly a surrealist, like André Breton. Heard of him? He's a poet, like my mum, only he started an art movement that led to some pretty crazy paintings that looked more like dreams than real life. That's why I'm a surrealist—because I'm stuck somewhere between dreams and real life. If only life wouldn't always stamp dreams out with its onward march.

Here's the three me's. At home I'm Joey, the unsporting, sometimes broody closet guitarist and older brother. At school I'm Joseph M. Green, the quiet kid who doesn't cause much trouble, but doesn't hold much interest, either.

That's all real life. But on the hill I'm the heroic, loud, sur-realist loner—ready and waiting for adventure, or at least for something to happen, or more specifically for some-thing to happen to me. I'm loud because I play my guitar there, and I play it without one bit of restraint. But that's where I live in my own dream.

The me I like the best is that me. The one who deals in dreams. The one on the hill, sitting on the grass as the sun sinks and the shadows are long and the world is far away. Everything glows then—trees, sky, ground, even me. Up there, I own the world. I get a waft of triumph. I'm playing my guitar and there's only the birds to hear me and only the sky to fill with notes. No one to snigger at me since, I admit it straight up, I'm no guitar hero. But at least up there I can imagine I am. Up there, I go about with a Jimi Hendrix swagger if I feel like it. I'm anything I want to be—famous astronaut, mountain climber, war-rior, poet. . . .

The sound of my guitar floats out over the hill, just like the coos of the wood pigeons do, or the puffs of winter woodsmoke, or the hoot of the train when it roars past. If I belong anywhere, it's to the hill and to the me that the hill brings out. The me who can strum those chords as long and loud as I like. But as you know, the sun sinks, the moment passes and I have to get home for dinner. I skulk out of my dream life and back into real life, where

I'm just plain awkward and unfitting. There I'm like a fish trying to walk on land.

When I get home, Dad is watering the vegetable garden.

"Hiya, Joey, where have you been?"

"Up the hill," I say. "With Black Betty," I add, just to make sense of my hill habit. Black Betty is our dog. Black as the night, of course, and partial to a walk, which makes her a perfect excuse and companion for my late-afternoon ventures. Dad is an odd-jobs man, which means he finds a way to earn a living in whatever way he can, when he isn't making sculptures in his shed. Making sculptures in his shed is what he prefers, but it doesn't pay the bills.

"Did you have a nice walk?"

"Yeah." This is typical of our conversations. Dad is sort of busy doing something, like watering the tomatoes, and with the other half of his mind he tries to show an interest in what I've been doing. But because I know he isn't really very interested in what I've actually been doing (playing guitar to the world), I never talk about it, and he believes instead that I have this not-very-exciting habit of taking Black Betty for a walk.

"How was school today?" he says, dropping the hose to pick some tomatoes.

"All right," I say. I tend to give up on these conversations before they have even started. What am I going to say? School is always kind of difficult, because I'm not really any good at anything and this makes me feel like a loser and then I act like a loser and once you get cast in the role of loser, even if it was you who cast yourself, no one wants to hang out with you. Except Digby, who for some reason accepts me, accepts the dull, unshining, defeated soursop me that I am at school. Digby is one of a kind, though. He's not impressed by the sporting stars. Not like Dad. You can't blame Dad, since he was one of those sporty types himself. He's athletic, he's got muscles and he's got skills. You should see him throw. We went for a swim at the reservoir last weekend. I was floating rather serenely, in my used car tire, dreaming about something. I was a long way away from the edge, where Dad was standing with Opal. But he threw a tennis ball at me and it made it all the way exactly to my hands. I still fumbled it. Dad shook his head, in despair, I think. But I dropped it partly 'cause I didn't believe it was possible to throw so far and to have such good aim, so I wasn't ready. I just get nervous anytime Dad tries to do something sporty with me. Sports isn't my thing. In fact, it's as if Dad and I come from different planets. I can only imagine how disappointing it is to have a son who you can't play catch with.

Dad hands me some tomatoes so he can get some leaves of basil. He knows better than to throw them to me. They'd be sauce before we got them to the kitchen.

"The good news is," he says, "I'm cooking pasta to-night."

It's not the best-ever news. The best-ever news would be that I suddenly grew muscles and could kick a football from one side of the oval to the other. Or I grew my real-life land legs and stopped feeling like a fish gasping on the playground, where real life plays itself out in ball games, good jokes, plain tomfoolery and bravado.

But Dad's pasta is pretty good, especially when it's cooked with homegrown tomatoes.

Schoolyard

I don't get back up the hill for weeks. There are two reasons for this.

First, Mr. Wratten, who wears small, round glasses, plays the fiddle and is one of the nicest teachers in the school, tells me I should join the chess club. I give it a go only because I wouldn't want to upset Mr. Wratten, which means I'm suddenly staying back after school in the chess headquarters, with all the other unsporty types, trying to learn how to be strategic. This is a futile attempt to uncover something I might be good at. As it turns out, I'm not really a strategic thinker, and instead of thinking three moves ahead, I am looking out the window and humming. To tell the truth, even if I turned out to be an undiscovered chess whiz, it's not really something I'm naturally drawn to. I really only keep at it to hang out with Max. Max is one of those kids who everyone likes and who like everyone. He just seems to be a small, red-headed dealer of good vibes. He aims them far and wide and everyone gives them back. It's what I call a happy circle. The fact that he laughs a lot and is always making everyone else laugh too helps circulate the happiness. Funny guys don't need to be sporty or geeky or cool; they're just likable. I'm playing a losing game of chess with Max, but who cares? We're playing.

"So I didn't know you liked chess, Joey," says Max.

"Yeah, I didn't know I liked it either—in fact, I'm still not sure," I say as Max takes one of my pawns.

"Well, you know what? If the computer beats you at chess every time, try kickboxing it. You'll probably win that one," says Max with a well-aimed grin.

"Don't bet on it. I'm a rank beginner as far as kickboxing goes," I say, and then I manage to take one of his pawns too.

What I like is playing, and playing anything with Max is fun. You may have gathered, I'm not one of the cool kids. I don't do jokes and I can't remember intriguing facts about the universe. You definitely wouldn't choose me for your team either, especially if it's a ball game, because balls, bats, hoops, hockey sticks and I have never hit it off. I bounced a football once, because my little sister, Opal, was trying to get me to play with her. It didn't grab me and I didn't grab it. Instead, it smashed Mum's terra-cotta pot of red geraniums and cost me a week's pocket money to replace it.

What I would like to play most of all with someone else is my guitar. In fact, I would say my very deepest wish is to one day be in a band. I mean it when I say it's deep—it's so deep down inside me I don't even let it surface. I'm way too shy to ever stand on a stage, let alone join a band. There is a guy in my class, Kenny Lopez. He's a drummer and he's in a band and they practice in the music room here at school. Kenny is like a sort of god to me. Not because he is godlike, but because he does what I dream of doing and he just takes it all in stride. I watch him going off to practice with his drumsticks, and it makes me all dreamy and envious at once. One lunchtime I sneak into the music room when no one is there to check it out, so I can imagine myself in there. There's a guitar leaning up against the piano stool, all alone, a shaft of sunlight slanted across it. It is like magic how I'm drawn to it: it's my gleaming pot of gold. I can't help sitting down and playing it. I have a tune in mind before I even realize it. I'm so absorbed that I don't even hear when someone comes to the door. I don't know how long he is there before I sense him and look up. It's one of the older kids; he looks friendly enough, but I stand up immediately and put the guitar down. I leave before he has a chance to say anything. I feel as if I've been caught with my hand in the biscuit tin.

Whereas Kenny, he just strolls in there without thinking.

After a week of my being thrashed at chess club, something else happens. I get chicken pox. Opal, my little sister, who is only seven and generally hogs the limelight and the trampoline, discovers them by jumping on me and trying to tickle under my shirt.

"Yuck, spots!" she yells.

I was wondering why I was feeling so lackluster.

I'm the ninth victim in the class. Already Kenny is down, and Max as well. In fact, I probably caught it playing chess with Max. It takes me a week to recover, a very slow, uneventful, itchy week. But once I'm well again, there is only one thing I'm itching to do.

Get back up the hill.

The Discovery

I've got my guitar and I'm going up my hill. I call it mine, but it's no one's hill. It's not even a real hill. Which is why I like it. A long time ago, it was just a tip at the end of a dirt road, and then they covered it with dirt, and once grass and other weeds grew, it looked like a hill. It's solitary, unremarkable, scruffy and unloved by almost everyone. The train screams right past it and no one inside even looks up.

The hill sure brings out the conqueror in me. Once I get on it, well, I stride up it, lofty as a cloud, my head stuffed with dreams. My faithful offsider, Black Betty, is always close by, snout to the ground, tail aloft and swashbuckling.

As soon as I'm here, I start dreaming. I imagine, for instance, that I am a famous explorer and am about to be interviewed on the radio. All the kids at school just happen to be listening.

But I hear a noise that doesn't belong, neither to the hill nor to my imagined interview. You wouldn't hear such banging in the middle of an interview with Sir Edmund Hillary. Heard of him? Sir Ed and Tenzing Norgay were the first guys to get to the top of Mount Everest. Not so many people talk about Tenzing Norgay, because he was from Tibet and he didn't get a knighthood.

There's the noise again. Louder. An invader?

High up in one of the peppercorns is what looks like a spaceship made by an amateur sort of builder. But as I get nearer, I see that it's a tree house. And now there is a frenzied rattling sound too.

Am I frightened?

Nope. I am Tenzing Norgay the mountaineer. I could even be Buzz Aldrin. Heard of him? He's an astronaut. The one who took the second steps on the moon.

I poke my head through the low-hanging branches.

What was once a quiet, hidden-away place, speckled with shafts of sunlight and the sharp smell of peppercorns, is now the grand entrance to someone's spaceship. The sides are made of corrugated tin, fence palings, an old gate and part of a table-tennis table. The roof is the rusted bonnet of a red Ford Falcon. All pieces of junk that have been lying around on the hill for ages, but it's the shape of a spaceship and, with all that tin, has an eerie silver gleam to it.

"Hey," I call out.

The banging stops instantly. There is no reply. Instead, an old pipe is thrust through a gap in one of the sides. It moves about until the eye clamped on the other end of it finds me. Black Betty's ears stand up and quiver.

An intruder. I knew I wouldn't like him.

"No need to spy," I say. "I'm Joey Green."

"Ajdye brishi."

I don't understand the words, but I know they are angry. The voice scratches the air. The words are fast and hard like bullets. I take a step closer. I want to hear the words instead of being hit by them. The pipe swings like an elephant's trunk and then droops downward. The spy scuttles. Is he afraid of me?

"Is that your name?" I say.

There is a pause.

Then a fierce shout: "No!"

The spy, hidden in his tree-house spaceship, is playing a game I don't understand.

I take a few more steps closer.

"Go away." Black Betty, who doesn't speak English or that other language, rushes forward and then stops. A hand—or is it a claw?—reaches out from beneath the car-bonnet roof and flings a small object, which I dodge quite expertly for someone who isn't blessed with nimble feet. I pick it up. It's a dog tag, a metal disc with engraved fancy letters: *Maude 0603 849 355*. I know Maude. She's a border collie who belongs to Molly, who lives on the other side of the hill. As I examine the dog tag, something hits me hard on the ear. The intruder has ammunition.

I crouch down this time, not taking my eyes off the tree house. Black Betty barks indignantly. I call out, "Hey, back off. That hurt."

Again the words fire. The same ones.

"Ajdye brishi."

Whatever it was that hit me glints on the ground. I grab it and stuff it in my pocket.

"Okay, okay, I'm going," I say. I can take a hint. I may have budding valor, but I'm not a warmonger. I'm all for peace and poetry.

I back out of the low-hanging branches and head home.

Halfway down the hill I put my hand in my pocket and take out the piece of ammunition. It's just an old AAA battery, speckled with rust. It doesn't tell me anything—at least, it doesn't tell me what I want to know. Who has taken over my hill? And why won't he show himself?

I shove the battery and the dog tag back in my pocket.

Maybe I'll give it back to Molly at school. Even though I set off down the hill, don't think I'm defeated. I've got plans to work out. This has only just begun.

Joey M. Green has a discovery to make and a hill to reclaim.

Joey M. Green

When something happens to me, even if it's only someone on my hill, I cling to it as if something about me, something special and not yet known, made it happen. Maybe I have a destiny after all.

I run the whole problem past Mum.

"Mum," I say, plonking myself by her. "What am I good at? I mean, what's my thing?"

I see her face as if it's in slow motion, as if I've thrown her a ball she can't catch. (Believe me, I know that feeling.) She makes all kinds of eye-popping, smile-wrenching contortions, and then her face falls into an apologetic half smile, as if she has let the whole team down.

"Well, darling, you're good at lots of things," she says finally.

I wait for her to list them.

"Like what?"

She sighs. "Well, for one thing, you're still only twelve years old. The best talents don't always surface easily; they take time to develop. I didn't write a poem until I was nineteen. And you're sensitive. You understand how others feel. You're nice. You're a nice kid, Joey."

I'm glad my mum likes me, but it's her job to do that, and being nice is nice, but nice is sort of drab—like a background color. It doesn't leap out at you. It definitely isn't the same as having a talent. It's not like being the best at something. Even a small thing would do—the fastest runner or the best at go-carts. Actually, go-carts, shmo-carts. That won't do. Maybe if I really have discovered an alien from space in that tree, the kids at school will be impressed. I'll walk around with the sort of swagger that famous people get on account of being talented, though not all famous people are talented nowadays. A lot of them are just good-looking, or rich, or relentless self-promoters. I'm none of the above, but I don't think I can rely on being the nice guy waiting quietly in the corner with a tissue for when you're upset about something. . . .

Maybe I'm Joey M. Green, explorer of the unknown. Discoverer of the long hidden. Seeker of things usually unsought. It's a name that could be not only remembered but revered by kids all over the world, all sorts of kids: sporty ones, spotty ones, geeky ones, quiet ones and quietly unremarkable ones.

Neil Armstrong probably never felt like he was waiting around with a tissue. Heard of him? He was the first guy ever to walk on the moon. He went there in a rocket with Buzz Aldrin. Everyone knows about Neil Armstrong because he got out of the rocket first, and then, on behalf of all mankind, which actually includes kids and women, he took the first steps on the moon. This happened way back in the olden days, sixteen years after Sir Ed and Tenzing climbed to the top of Mount Everest. I know because I googled it. I wasn't exactly meaning to google it; I just typed in the words *first man* and it comes up with *first man on the moon,* then *first man in space,* then *first man to climb Mount Everest.* Nowhere do I see *first man with sensitivities.* Nowhere do I see *first nice man.* Because, let's face it, landing on the moon and climbing unclimbable mountains on behalf of all mankind are deadly important and a million times more glorious and triumphant than being nice or sensitive.

I wonder what went on inside the rocket between Buzz Aldrin and Neil Armstrong after they landed on the moon. Did they pull straws to see who got to take the first step? Or did it come to fisticuffs? Or did they work it out like gentlemen? Did Buzz Aldrin say, *After you, Neil. I'll be content to be the second man to walk on the moon*? Was Buzz just a nice guy (with sensitivities) and was it because of that niceness that he will forever be known as the second man to walk on the moon? Or barely be remembered at all? Maybe Neil purposefully sat nearest the door because he was determined to be the first man from the outset. Is that the sort of grit you need if you are going to make a mark? Because that's the kind of grit I don't have.

But now the hill has its very own mystery on top. Discovered by me, Joey M. Green—a name with the same rhythm as Muhammad Ali. Heard of him? He was an American boxer, one of the greatest heavyweights ever, and he wasn't just a sports star; he stood up for freedom and justice too. Important stuff. He was no lightweight.

What Mum doesn't realize is that her son may be the first to discover an alien. I don't tell her; I just fairly swagger out into the garden instead.

"Hey, watch this, Joey," Opal says as she does a somersault on the trampoline. She lands on her feet and springs up in the air like a champion, because she knows it was good and she knows I can't do somersaults. Opal is one big show-off.

I'm not swaggering anymore. I'm standing still with my hands shoved in my pockets. I'm standing here, small in our big garden. It's lucky there is no one else here, actually.

Our garden is full of weed-choked flower beds and large old trees, two shaggy palms that stand at the front of the house looking like two old punks. At the moment our grass is yellow, as it's late summer and no one waters it. The trampoline, big and unnetted with exposed springs like bare bones, is where kids hang out. Because it sits beneath the elm tree, it's shaded in summer, and it's a place to jump to from the tree platform that my dad built. He attached a sliding-up-and-down pole, a basketball hoop and a ladder to it. So quite a few kids (Ezra and Pippa Jay, Sam, Louis, Charlie and Jemima) hang around in our garden. They all meet on the tramp or the platform, eat snacks, have water fights, lie about and talk or just jump around on the tramp. Opal does somersaults and other stunts on it. For some kids the trampoline is as good as a hill. Not for me, though.

"Where were you before?" Opal has forgotten her somersault already. She hates it when I go out without her. She wants to know everything I'm doing and then she wants to do it too. It's her version of love. She tries to attach herself to me and I try to shake her off. That's probably why she learned to bounce so well.

"Just walking Black Betty up the hill," I say. I'm not going to tell her anything about the tree house or the strange person inside it. Opal can keep her somersaults and I'll keep my discovery.

Opal shrugs. She squats down and throws her arms around Black Betty, but she is looking at me. She thinks I can't tell. She thinks she is camouflaged within Black Betty.

She is checking for withholdings. Opal has a sixth sense about things. I do too. It's something we have in common. We get it from our mum, who is a poetry teacher, which these days makes her out of a job.

Can Opal tell I have a secret? I lean back on my heels and do my best to hide my thoughts. But Opal has already moved on. She never cares about anything for long. She suddenly releases Black Betty and races inside, yelling over her shoulder, "Anyway, Dad is making pizza. It's movie night."

Friday night is pizza-and-movie night. All of us on the couch—me, Opal, Mum, Dad and Black Betty—and Oscar the cat curled in a handsome bundle on the armchair. It's pretty cozy and especially nice because the next day is Saturday, which means no school. And now I have a plan for tomorrow. I'm going back up my hill to investigate the tree house and its unfriendly inhabitant.

After pizza and the movie, you'll find me in my bedroom mucking around on my guitar. Don't even think about Jimi Hendrix—I only know five chords. Think of Frankie Facini, who is just some young kid who sings and plays guitar outside the fruit shop. He's already a lot better than me. If you put me outside the fruit shop, I would just die.

5

The Tiny Things

At breakfast, Mum says, "Who is coming to the market?" She says this every Saturday morning. No one ever wants to go. Opal will go if she gets an apple Danish, though lately she tries for a cupcake with pink icing, which Mum says is full of chemicals that will make you hyperactive. Opal is already hyperactive—she will probably be an Olympic gymnast one day. She eyes me, waiting to see if I have a better option. But I have grim, jealous feelings and a do-not-enter-here look.

Dad gives Mum a pacifying rub on the shoulders and says he has jobs to do—a plausible excuse given that he is an odd-jobs man. Dad can fix anything, even Mum's shoulders. He's got what he calls fix-it hands.

"Joey, will you come?" says Mum hopefully.

Opal watches me.

"Homework," I lie, and shrug for effect.

"On Saturday? You shouldn't have to do homework on the weekend," Mum mutters to herself. She doesn't really care who comes. She loves the market. It's all about atmosphere for her. "Come on, Opal. I'll get you an apple Danish," she says.

Opal considers her options. With me and Dad busy, the market is her best bet. "The one with icing?" Opal bargains anyway.

Mum sighs. She can't be bothered having an argument about it. "All right. Come on, then." She plonks a sun hat on Opal, takes her hand, and off they go.

That leaves the coast clear for my investigations. I have already considered all possible plans of attack, though attack is really not my game. I hope to find the tree house unattended and simply scope out the joint. But if it is occupied, a peace offering is what I've got in mind.

At first I wondered if a blueberry muffin might do the job, but muffins probably only work on sugar-starved kids like Opal and me. Maybe a better peace offering would be a small metal object, something like the ones he threw at me. Even though they weren't used in peace, this would really show some admirable goodwill on my part, which, after all, is supposedly my specialty.

I hunt around the house, but it's harder than you would think to find something with the right sort of weight, size and availability—that is, something that isn't already being used, like Mum's guitar slide or Dad's key ring.

In the end I go into Dad's shed. Dad is there, of course. He's making a huge winged man. It's for a sculpture prize. He's making it mostly out of wood, but the wings are copper wire. He's working on the backbone—head down, a whining saw, wood dust in the air. He stops when I come in.

"Hey, Joey."

"Hi, Dad."

He smiles and wipes the wood shavings off the bench. He knows I want something.

I'm not sure how to put it. I should have figured it out before I went in. "I need to find a small metallic sort of object. Do you have something I can use?" I ask.

"This shed is pretty much overrun with small metallic objects. What do you want it for?" he says.

"Well, it's not for any particular use. Not to build something, just for a collection. A project. You know, a school thing."

"Oh, a science project. Are you looking at metals?"

"No, not science. More like drama. We're staging a war. We need old-fashioned ammunition." I'm terrible at lying. And I don't like it either. So I have to get it as close as possible to the truth or I'll trip up for sure.

Dad nods. I can see he is thinking it over, doing his

best to find a solution. He takes down a couple of boxes off the shelves. They are full of screws, nuts, bolts and washers. A gold mine.

"How about these? And what about a shield? You and I could knock one out. You'd need a shield, I reckon. We could make it out of wood with a metal band at the back to put your arm through."

Dad keeps suggesting that we make something together, even though every time I try to use a tool, whatever I make comes out wonky. Dads and their sons are meant to bond over these sorts of activities, wielding hammers or kicking footies. Sometimes I wish that instead of me always feeling like I can't speak Dad's language, he would try and understand mine. But he doesn't. He doesn't understand me because he doesn't rate music: it's too abstract, it doesn't earn a living, it doesn't fix anything and it isn't something you can win at. Instead, he keeps trying to show me how to hammer a nail. He has natural enthusiasm for my pretend project because it involves tools, or he thinks it does. All I want is one small nut or bolt, and only to give away, and now I'm going to end up with a homemade wooden shield. Weirdly, a shield might be exactly what I do need, in case I'm attacked again, but I can't talk to Dad about that, because he wouldn't understand why I would even want to win over a hill intruder. He doesn't even know how important the hill is to me. Hills, music, songs, the real surrealist me—these are all secret and special nouns in a language my dad doesn't speak.

"Dad, this is perfect for now. I'll take this bolt and I'll talk to the guys and see if a shield would be good." I consider telling him how much I like his winged sculpture, but I don't. My opinion isn't really worth much. I bet he thinks I don't even notice anything that's made with tools.

"Sure thing," he says. I can see he's a little disappointed.

Maybe I will let him make me a shield, but not now. Now I have to go back up the hill before the alien leaves.

I have the three things in my pocket. The battery, the dog tag and a bolt. Black Betty is trotting alongside me. The sky is blue, cloudless and bright. The air is warm but not stinking hot. It's a perfect day for encountering.

Encountering what? A Martian? An alien invader of hills? I like to imagine that everything is possible, even if it isn't. Explorers shouldn't squish down their curiosity with the weight of probability.

I press on, checking for signs. This time there is no banging, just the twitter of small birds. A couple of woodies fly overhead. The air whooshes in their wings. Old Grey, the lone kangaroo who has been kicked out of the mob by the young bucks, is nowhere to be seen. But the tree-house spaceship is there looking dazed and perilous, as if it arrived in the tree with an unexpected jolt and is still slightly alarmed.

I edge closer. Black Betty stays low. We slide under the hanging peppercorn branches. I stand very still and listen. Black Betty sniffs around. There are no signs of life coming from the tree house. I call out, "Hey! Anybody home?"

No answer.

I go right up to the trunk. There are small wooden struts nailed into it. Whoever made this house must know a bit about building, but not nearly as much as my dad. My dad could teach him a thing or two.

I gaze up. The trunk leads to a gap in the floor, which I figure is the entrance. I begin my climb. Black Betty barks; she is annoyed she can't come too.

"I won't be long. Don't worry," I call out.

Now that I'm on the way up, I feel like I'm trespassing. I pop my head through the gap in the floor and look around. I feel like a snoop. I *am* trespassing. I feel as if I've broken into someone else's home. Only this is not really a home. Or a tree house. It's more like a sort of theater. A place of wonder.

On the ends of all the thinnest branches there are tags of aluminum foil, which shower flecks of light in the breeze. Three wooden shelves, nailed to the tree trunk, hold an array of things, including an old-fashioned phone with a dial, and there are all sorts of tiny objects on the floor, right at my eye level. They seem to have been placed with some mysterious purpose, as if someone was playing a chess game on the floor. And in the middle of all of them is a wooden stool. It looks like a giant in a world of tiny creatures.

The tiny things are just normal, everyday things—a thimble, a button, a pencil sharpener, an acorn, a coin, a binder clip, a washer, a stone, an elastic band, a bobby pin, a plug. They look as if they are in the middle of a game. There is a tooth, and next to it, as if in conversation with it, is an acorn. Fanning out around a belt buckle like children listening to the teacher are a periwinkle shell, a bottle lid and a silver button. Directly in front of the sharpener, and placed as if in confrontation, is a die. Is it a duel?

The more I look around, the more objects I notice. A yo-yo hangs from a thin branch, and below it is a jar lid full of water. A key ring is tied to another branch with a hair tie, and next to it a beaded earring dangles as if taunting the key ring with its attractiveness.

I hoist myself inside and, avoiding the little things on the floor, examine the other objects on the shelves above the phone. There's a terra-cotta pot full of birdseed, a tiny basket full of dried red rose petals and some books: *What*

Bird Is That?, something in another language and *How to Build Treehouses, Huts and Forts* by David Stiles. I pull this one down.

It's a large, well-thumbed book full of drawings and instructions on how to build structures. There are pages folded over and marks in the margin. It's a book that is so well used it feels ancient. Inside it there is a design for a lookout tower based on one used by George Washington. Heard of him? The first-ever president of the United States of America. A very famous man. Someone has taught himself how to build this place. I'm begrudgingly impressed.

"Hey."

It's the voice. That sharp wind of a voice from yesterday. I've been caught. I look out over the wall.

I see the spaceship builder, the hill occupier, the collector of small things.

It's a girl. She stares at me with eyes of fire. She's small, with a bundle of hair as black as ink, khaki overalls and bare feet. She's got a wild look, and she narrows her eyes at me as if she wants to kill me. But then she gives a tiny, dismissive jerk of her head and ducks out of the tree branches.

Before I have time for my peace offering, she has disappeared.

A Battleground

I've invaded her space. But she invaded mine too. So we're even.

She didn't act like we were even. She looked at me as if I was just a piece of rubbish. But before she turned away, I saw a sadness ripple across her face, like a wind across a lake. It made me sorry that I'd invaded her spaceship.

I'd like to climb down and try to find her. But I don't do it. I don't know why. I don't know what I would say. If I said something like *I'm sorry for being in your space, but actually you are on my hill,* then she would say, *It's not your hill.* And she'd be right. She wouldn't understand the ways of the hill. There is no point explaining that the hill is Not for Dwelling On. That it's meant to be roamed over. As I do. As Old Grey does. As Black Betty does. And the rabbits, snakes and wood pigeons do. But who can understand that?

I jiggle the small metal objects I have in my pocket. I might be in her tree house, but at least I didn't throw stuff at her. I even brought back her battery and the dog tag. And I brought her another piece for her collection. The more I think about it, the more I agree with myself that we are even, or at least that I am not the bad guy.

Although maybe it's not so bad to be the bad guy. It's better than being the sensitive guy. Bad guys have a brooding, suspenseful allure. I give a heedless bad-guy shrug, a who-cares-about-that-wild-girl-anyway sort of a shrug.

It's not right, though. My shoulders aren't careless shruggers. They're cautious, seeking-out shoulders, and I can't help worrying about that wild girl. Apparently, if you touch eggs in a nest, the mother bird won't come back. I feel as if I have ruined the Martian girl's special nest with its tiny creatures and, just like a mother bird, she won't return.

I put the book back on the shelf. I take my three offerings—battery, bolt and dog tag—and place them in a row on the floor. But they look useless, misplaced. I sit the battery up on its end, I stand the bolt next to it and then I balance the dog tag on top of them. Now they look like they belong. Not everyone could have done this. It required sensitivity.

I climb down from the tree. Will she be hiding somewhere, waiting for me to leave? I walk down to the pines and lie on my back in the shade. Black Betty lies down too. I watch her, how she lies, listening, with one ear open to the world, the other sighing forward.

I close my eyes. Sounds waft over me: birdcalls, the cars humming in the distance, shouts and the clod of balls on bats from the oval down the hill—Saturday-morning cricket. I hear my own quiet sigh. Boys from my class will be there. Probably Kip Walker and Amos Reed— those sporty guys. They'll be down there with their proud dads. My dad isn't proud of me like that. Not that he has ever said he wishes I played cricket, but he must think it sometimes. How can a dad be proud of a kid who never stands out?

Who cares about cricket? There is more to life than swiping at hard red balls that come hurtling down a pitch. Life is full of intrigue: planets, mysteries, forests, mythic heroes, music—even the wild girl.

What does she do in her tree house with those small objects? I want to know, but how can I find out when she won't talk to me? I don't think anyone has ever disliked me before. I'm not popular, but no one actively dislikes me. I don't make enough of an impression to be disliked. If I was a bump on the road, you wouldn't even trip over me.

Max and Digby aren't on the cricket team either. Max probably could be if he wanted, but he doesn't try very hard at things. As I said, he's here for a laugh. If he sees a horse, he walks up to it and says, "Why the long face?" and cracks himself up. Digby is lanky and straggly, and if he runs, he looks like a gorilla, arms swinging, legs lolloping. He makes me look outright athletic. He's brainy, though, and he's into insects. He'll start talking about caterpillars or killer wasps at any moment.

Then there's the gang, the other guys. They're the ones everyone wants to be friends with. That's Kenny Lopez, who, I already told you, can play the drums, and Raffie Langslow, who is a skater and who all the girls go crazy for, and Harry Jay, who is mad about footy and has five sisters. There is also Pim Wilder, who isn't actually in the gang, but just hangs out with whoever is doing something interesting at the time. Who would I be if I was in the gang? I could be the sensitive guy. But gangs don't need sensitivities. They need grit.

Something makes me sit up. Maybe it was Black Betty. Her sleeping ear is now angled to attention. I turn around. There, above me on the hill, is the Martian girl.

This time she doesn't run away.

I scramble to my feet.

We lock eyes. Her gaze is curious, but wary. She steps back. Her weight shifts. She seems ready to run.

I smile. It's an instinct I have. A big, dumb instinct. When I'm lost for what to do or say, I just smile.

She doesn't smile back, but her mouth softens. She

drops to a squat and holds out her hand. It is clasped shut, but she fans it open and my bolt rolls out and onto the ground. She flings me a stern, contemptuous look and folds her arms, like a proud hunter who just speared her prey. And then she turns and marches back up the hill.

Peace Offerings

I have the bolt in my sock drawer. I don't know what to do with it. Every time I open the drawer, it rolls about dejectedly. Can a bolt be dejected? Ever since the Martian girl rejected it, I have been feeling like even more of an outcast.

I don't even know her. She's not a friend, and she might not have anything interesting to say at all. But when the bolt rolled out of her palm and landed on the dirt, it was as if a piece of me landed in the dirt, the goofy, smiling face of friendship that I had offered.

If I was Max, I would have just laughed when she did that. If I was Digby, I would make sense of it somehow. They wouldn't mope, like I am. And they won't even notice the quandary this has thrown me into. I am the noticer of feelings.

*   *   *

By the time Monday comes, I've pulled myself together. As usual, as soon as the bell for lunch goes, Harry walks straight past me, slouches over the desk toward Kenny Lopez and says, "Want to kick the footy?"

Kenny says, "Nuh, I'm going to the music room."

Kenny can say this. He can be asked to join in and say no, 'cause it's no big deal for him. I can't imagine this. If anyone asked me to have a kick, I'd do it, just to join in. But they never ask me.

"Huh? Music at lunchtime?" Harry can't understand it.

"Yeah. I'm practicing with Hamish. The Battle of the Bands is coming up."

The Battle of the Bands is a big night. It's like a practice run for the sort of night real bands have, without parents and with beer. At the Battle of the Bands there is no beer and plenty of parents, but still, it's dark, it's loud and it's rock. Everyone goes. Everyone tries to look as cool as hell. If I go, I just try to look like I'm not too interested, since if anyone was ever going to get a hint of my deepest, most secret dream, it would be there, when it might float to the surface and I could be caught all misty-eyed and accidentally yearning to be in one of the bands.

I glance at Kenny Lopez. A small, uncool voice in me whispers, *But I get it—I like music.* I hope he can hear it, but he can't, no matter how loudly I think it.

Harry Jay is already rounding up some others. Kenny Lopez is getting his drumsticks out of his locker. He sits for a moment and drums the desk with them.

I want to tell him that I play guitar.

I stand up. He doesn't even look at me. I push my chair back so it squeaks on the floor. He looks up, but you can tell he has a song in his head and he is drumming along to it. He stops suddenly and grins at me, and then he leaves. He's not bad, Kenny Lopez. I'll cheer for him at the Battle of the Bands. Maybe if I hadn't already been rejected by the Martian girl, I might have casually mentioned that I play guitar. But probably not. It's not really worth mentioning, since I'm not good enough to play in front of anyone other than Black Betty.

After school Digby and I always walk part of the way home together. We go by the creek.

I half want to tell him about what happened on the hill, but I'm embarrassed. Being upset about a girl you don't even know who rejected your present of a small metal bolt would be a big joke if it got out. There would be high-voltage ridicule.

So I start like this: "What would you do if someone put a curse on you?"

Digby looks at me to check I haven't gone bonkers. Digby believes in scientific facts—the hexagonal cells of beehives, the silken trails of caterpillars, the toothed forearm of a praying mantis.

I shrug. "Just imagining," I say, flippantly.

"Did you eat some cactus or something?" Digby cranes his neck toward me like a giraffe. He looks worried.

"No, I try not to eat cactus at school," I say. This isn't getting me where I want to go. I try another tack. "You know when Captain Cook first arrived in Australia, did he try to give the Aboriginal people something as a peace offering? It was their land, their trees he was cutting down, their fish he was eating."

"Their turtles, you mean? Cook's sailors ate all the turtles!" Digby enthuses. He's keen on turtles. Then he shakes his head. His voice comes out in a long, exasperated sigh. "They didn't think about breeding seasons—if you eat all the turtles, there won't be any next year. No wonder the Aborigines got angry."

This is the sort of interesting fact that Digby knows, but turtles are not my main concern. I persist with my problem in disguise: "If someone invades someone else's land and then disrespects the ways of the place, or if one person tries to make peace by offering a gift and the other one rejects it, that's like declaring war, isn't it? Who owns the moon, for instance, the first people to land there, or the first people to care for it and dwell there?"

"No one owns the moon." Digby shrugs. "Why the sudden interest in history?"

"It's not history. It's now too. Two different sorts of people meet, for instance. One speaks one language and the other speaks a different one. One feels it is their land since their stories have all happened there, but the other is sitting there making their own stories up at the same time. And then, bang, misunderstanding all around." I'm imagining the letter I would leave at the Martian girl's spaceship, if I was more of a mean person.

> *If you left the hill now, I wouldn't care. In fact,*
> *Black Betty and me and everyone else, including*
> *the woodies, snakes, rabbits and dog walkers who*
> *understand the ways of the hill, none of us would*
> *care two hoots if you flew up into space in your*
> *honky wooden spaceship. We might even be relieved.*

Digby is completely perplexed. He stares at me as if I am turning primitive. Maybe I am. Maybe I have tapped into the anger of all those who have been invaded before me. Maybe it is my path to fight for the oppressed, the downgraded, the invaded, the rejected. . . . Maybe these are the world's gentle people.

It's hard trying to speak to Digby in code. He thinks in facts. But I like to think in poems, or clouds. He thinks about probabilities; I think about possibilities. But somehow we arrive at a similar place in the end. Usually.

"Hey, you want to go see if we can find that turtle in the creek? Or we could get some tadpoles for Opal," I suggest.

Digby's face breaks into a smile. "Last time we got taddies, your cat ate them." Digby is laughing to himself. He is walking faster. He is relieved that our talk has returned to things that wriggle and grow and transform exactly as they are meant to. For Digby, that's all we need.

And sometimes I think that too. Who needs the Martian girl?

Roar, Lion of the Heart

Mum writes out poems and sticks them on the fridge. Not her own poems, just poems she likes. After school, when I go to the fridge to get the milk for my Weet-Bix, there is a new one.

> *You that come to birth and bring the mysteries,*
> *Your voice-thunder makes us very happy.*
> *Roar, lion of the heart,*
> *And tear me open.*
>
> —RUMI

Like I said, Mum is a bit supernatural. She senses things. She is always standing there looking at something, getting the sense of it. She is standing in the doorway looking at me in that way now.

"Joey, do you want to go for a walk?" she says, as if she knows what I want or need more than I do.

I do want to go for a walk. But I can't go up the hill without feeling like I'm going to battle. The wild girl has turned the hill into a place to be fought for. But I'm not going to accept defeat either. I may be a nice guy, but I'm not a quitter.

I'm striding up the hill. I may not have much, but I've got something. Gall? Readiness? Determination? Courage? Did Burke and Wills have that? Heard of them? They were the explorers who are famous for not making it. Funny thing to be famous for. Though they don't know this, of course, as they died along the way. Somewhere between Melbourne and the Gulf of Carpentaria, they died of starvation and beriberi.

Apparently, Burke, who was the leader, foolishly shot at some Aborigines who would otherwise have given him seedcakes. Poor Wills. What could be worse than being second in command to an incompetent leader on a failed expedition and dying while you're at it?

Speaking of second in command, I've got Black Betty bounding beside me. I would have had Opal too, but I got her off my trail by showing her Mum's chocolate stash in the desk drawer. It was a hard secret to give up, but that just shows how determined I am.

This time I approach the tree house with stealth. Not because I'm afraid, but because I need to be alert, ready for anything—it could be bombardment with small, hard objects, or it could be just a plain but gutting attack of meanness. I have to be strong inwardly and outwardly too. Ready.

Roar, lion of the heart.

There is a path that leads around and up the hill. It's yellow dirt with white quartz stones that gleam rough and hot. On the right of it, where the slope is cut into for the railway track, the hill falls away to a tangle of scrub, gorse, wattle and grasses. On the left is the sweeping mound of the hill, straw-colored, blanketed in weeds and scattered with peach and nectarine trees and hollyhock in spring when it all turns green again. I am creeping up the left side, which means if she's in the tree house, she won't see me coming.

I can hear a sound that is so soft I am almost under the tree branches before I can tell what it is.

It's singing, as pretty and melodic as a bird's.

She is singing.

I picture her lying on her back gazing up at the leaf-dappled sky, enjoying her empire in the trees, singing to the sky. Her voice is so much sweeter than she is. The song is tuneful but strange. It's old-fashioned and in another language. It's not in Spanish either. (I know because we learn Spanish at school.) In fact, there is nothing familiar about it, not the words or the melody or the way she is singing it. She sings as if her song is a dream.

I stand still to consider this. Martian Girl is a puzzle that doesn't make sense to me. I have to get her to talk to me. I make my way quietly and stand beneath the tree house. I don't know what I want, maybe just to work out who she is. Or to show her that I am . . . whatever it is I am.

I climb up the wooden struts. The singing continues. I put my head through the opening.

She sees me the same moment I see her. She is crouched down on her knees, but she sits up, startled, and swallows her song whole.

She doesn't shout at me. She doesn't turn fierce at all. Her whole face opens, as if something wondrous has happened, and she stares at me as if I'm a long-lost friend returned. Then she blinks and drops her gaze. In her palm is an acorn, and she holds it tenderly, as if she has been soothing it with her song.

She says, without looking at me, "We've been expecting you."

9

The Plains of Khazar

Who does she mean? Who is expecting me? Have I walked into a trap?

"We?" I ask.

"Yes, we." She sweeps her hand toward the floor, where her strange game is set out. "Us," she says.

Us? She isn't kidding. I can see she expects me to enter her game.

I'm sort of used to this. Because of Opal. Opal does it with her friends. They wear old hats and pink wire wings, and they build palaces in the wormwood bush, make potions out of calendula petals and invent worlds where they are queens. If you happen to see them while they are in that world, you have to play along. It's only fair with little kids.

But Martian Girl isn't a little kid.

I don't know what to say. I'm not sure I want to be a

part of her game. But I feel like if I say the wrong thing, I will ruin the game, and I do want to make peace, after all. If I ask her to explain, that would be like breaking the spell. I've read enough fairy tales to know that. And Martian Girl is a bit like someone in a fairy tale. She wears a rust-colored dress that's way too big for her and a sky-blue-spotted tie for a belt. Around her neck is a sea-worn pebble on a piece of string, and her feet are bare. Her hair is as black as night and her skin is pale—she is half day, half night. She doesn't look like an alien, but she looks like more than a girl.

"Okay, so introduce me," I say. "Like I said the other day, I'm Joey."

She gives a sly smile of approval. Then lifts her nose in a superior way.

"Not everyone is ready to be introduced. Names are private. You give yours too fast."

Too fast? A name is a name. Why make mysteries out of simple things? This is why girls make me squirm. I try again.

"What were you singing?"

Her eyebrows lift. She is surprised I heard her but she shows no embarrassment. I get the feeling her singing is private, but not in a shameful way like my guitar playing. She leans forward, glues her gaze on me as hard as she can and whispers, "I am singing them down."

"Singing who down?"

She flicks her head, glancing down at the small things, then back to me.

We stare at each other. I expected her to be secretive or proud, but this is just strange. I have no idea what she means.

"Down from where?" I ask.

She nods up toward the blue sky. "From the Plains of Khazar."

"The Plains of Khazar?" I repeat. It seems I have landed in a fairy tale.

"It's where Mumija is." She picks up the acorn between her thumb and forefinger and shows it to me. "This is Mumija."

I don't know what to say.

"There! You have a name now," she declares. "Mumija. She is the queen. She protects you from storms. From loneliness."

She whispers this last word. *Loneliness.* It's as if she didn't want me to hear it. She quickly looks away.

I lean closer. "When you say you sing them down, what do you mean? Aren't they already here?"

She shakes her head. "No, I sing them down from the Plains of Khazar."

I can't hide the fact that I'm still perplexed. She rolls her eyes.

"The songs are their songs, the people who live on the plains. When I sing their songs, the people come to me. If you sing an Elvis Presley song, can't you see him?"

She doesn't wait for an answer; she jumps up and, as if none of this has happened, pushes her hands up toward the Ford Falcon–bonnet roof.

"Can you help me, please? I need someone to hold it here while I hammer in this nail."

The Plains of Khazar have vamoosed. She has closed the door on her fairy tale.

I stand up and help her heave the roof toward the trunk of the tree, where she has nailed some wooden struts to support it. I have to watch where I stand to avoid knocking over any of the small things.

"Do all of these things have names?" I ask.

She hammers a nail and frowns. "Of course they do. You have a name. Everything does."

"What's the tree's name?" It occurs to me that maybe she is right. Maybe I just haven't thought about this before.

"I don't know everything's name. What's his name?" She points down at Black Betty, who is curled up at the bottom of the trunk.

"She's Black Betty."

She gazes down at Black Betty and calls her name. "You're lucky to have a dog. I just have the birds."

"What birds?" I say.

She stares up into the tree. "All of them: the little crows, the wood swallows, the white-winged choughs and magpies. I've even seen a pair of rose robins. Their nests are made of lichen and moss and they're lined with fur and bound with cobwebs. If I was very small, that's where I'd sleep."

"Which school do you go to?"

"I don't go to school. I learn everything here."

"I thought everyone had to go to school."

"Who says? I make up my own mind."

"Don't your parents tell you to go to school?"

She turns away from me and stares out over the hill. Her arms rest on the side of the tree house. I guess she makes up her own mind about what she wants to talk about too.

I stare out through the peppercorn branches to the sky and the curve of the hill and the tops of the town's houses. It's still my hill. But maybe it can be hers as well. I haven't decided.

For a while we don't say anything. It feels okay to say nothing. Usually silence between people makes me uncomfortable, but with her it's different. She doesn't seem to care whether I speak or not. I like it. I like the feeling of being in a game, of not knowing what to believe. I can be Muhammad Ali. I can be Neil Armstrong.

Maybe I can walk on the Plains of Khazar.

"Do you need any help?" I ask. "I've got lots of stuff at home that you could use. I mean, did you build this on your own? Did someone help you?"

I'm imagining raiding my dad's shed. In an instant I have switched from resenting her and her strange tree house to wanting to help her finish it. So much for my speech about not owning the hill.

She pushes the side of her building to show its stability. It's not really very stable at all, but I don't mention this.

"No one helped me. I taught myself how to build it from a book. The hardest thing was finding all the stuff and getting it here. It took me a long time."

"Where did you get the tools?"

"I know someone. He has a shed full of stuff. He let me have them."

I can tell she is lying. She isn't looking at me. She is frowning into the distance. I figure now is not the right time to talk about lying. Maybe I'm wrong, anyway.

"Why did you build a tree house? It's a big project to do on your own."

She turns to me. "A tree house?" She scoffs and shakes her head. "This is not a tree house."

"It looks like a spaceship."

"It's not a spaceship, either."

"What is it, then?"

She looks confused. Either she has never really thought about what it is or she isn't ready to disclose the secret purpose she has for it. She turns back to stare out over the hill.

"It's halfway to Khazar," she says. "It's a platform. So I can reach the clouds. I have a wind telephone too."

"A wind telephone?"

"Yes, the wind carries the voices down to me, and I speak through the phone."

She turns toward me, drawing herself up. It's as if she is trying to make herself bigger, more believable. "If you want to help me, you can bring me some food. Bread and Nutella. My dad never buys stuff like that. That's what I want. Why don't you sing?"

"I don't know," I say. I'm perplexed. How does she know I don't sing? And what has singing got to do with this cloud platform? Or the wind telephone?

She shrugs. "So I'll teach you. You bring me some food; I'll bring you some songs. Deal?" She holds out her hand to shake.

I don't want to sing, and I'm not really one for making deals, but I shake on it anyway. For her sake.

I turn to leave and then remember I don't even know her name. But I have an idea.

"Hey, I've been calling you Martian Girl, because your tree house looks like a spaceship. Can I call you Marsh for short? I have to call you something."

I don't tell her that even though I knew the chance of a Martian spacecraft visiting Earth was minuscule, I still wanted to imagine it was possible. She certainly doesn't let reality get in the way of her ideas.

"Marsh?" She says the word and tilts her head, as if trying it on for size. She acts nonchalant, but I can see she is pleased. She likes it. She holds out her hand to shake again, as if this is also a deal.

"Well, if I'm a Martian, that makes this hill Mars, so see you tomorrow, Joey Planet Walker," she says.

"See ya, Marsh."

Where We All Fit

At home, Mum is making dinner. She is peeling a sweet potato. Opal and Dad are playing cards.

"Nice walk, Joey?" Mum is checking, since it was her idea for me to go for a walk.

"She's making salad again," says Opal, screwing up her face in disgust. Mum often makes elaborate salads, as she calls them. Opal hates them, elaborate or not. Opal won't eat anything that isn't cooked and at least partially covered with cheese. It's a constant battle between her and Mum. Mum sneaks lettuce leaves into Opal's cheese sandwiches. Opal pulls the cucumber out of her nori rolls.

"Snap!" says Dad, slamming his hand on the card pile.

"Oh nooo!" cries Opal, slumping on the table. "I lost concentration."

"Just the thought of cucumber and you're a goner," I say, keeping the conversation away from my walk. I don't want to tell anyone about Marsh yet. I sort of like the secret. It makes me feel like I've got something special going on that needs privacy if it's going to grow in any way. If I say anything about my walk, Mum will see that I'm covering up something—she always does. And then it will be out. Best to steer the talk away from the walk.

"What's Opal having?" I ask. Opal usually ends up with something different if it's elaborate salad for dinner.

"Cheese omelet!" Opal beams.

For me, a cheese omelet and an elaborate salad are pretty equal, though possibly because I sort of suffer all the salad stuff in the hope that it will make me tough and sporty or give me some other heroic quality. Nothing so far. Still, I hear it takes a lot of greens and you have to chew them well.

I go to the fridge to get Black Betty her meat-and-oat mash for dinner, and also to see what food I could get for Wild Girl. For Marsh. As soon as I say it like that in my head, it sounds like I know her, like Digby or Max.

Marsh.

The truth is, we don't have Nutella here. If we did, Opal would just eat it all up when no one was looking. We have peanut butter and honey. So either I buy some Nutella or I just take her some peanut-butter-and-honey sandwiches instead. I could make myself extra for lunch tomorrow. No one would notice.

Does she want Nutella or is she just hungry and Nutella came to mind? She is pretty skinny, but so am I, and that's just the way I am—it's not because I'm hungry.

But Marsh could be hungry. She could be anything. She could be completely crazy or a fine actor or wildly imaginative or really living in another reality. I can't tell, but I'm interested to find out.

What does Marsh like? Digby is a straight shooter: it's all bugs and creatures, the wonders of the natural world. I admire that. He's not influenced by what everyone else thinks. It's not cool to be into insects, but he doesn't care. He sees the other guys almost as if they are insects. He watches them with distant curiosity, and then he walks along the creek and hunts for dragonflies. Whereas I walk past the music room at school, where Kenny and the guys are rehearsing for the Battle of the Bands, and I look in with intense yearning, and then I walk on, acting as casual as anything, when really I'm churned up.

But Marsh . . . I get the feeling Marsh isn't even looking at anyone else. Marsh is in her own world. Marsh even makes her own world—a world of clouds and wind and birds and small things.

I don't like to wonder about where we all fit. It's like imagining yourself in a big race with every kid you know, and no matter which way you picture it, you aren't winning; you aren't even in the running. In fact, you gave up early on, kicked off your running shoes, hung them over your shoulder and walked away, acting like you didn't care, anyway, because some part of you really didn't care.

But some part of you did. And the part of you that did care is kicking the part of you that didn't care, and the part that didn't care just wants to wake up in the sun and not worry about anything.

The Return

At school, Pim Wilder told the class that 11 percent of the world's population is left-handed. He also tied a papier-mâché angel with cockatoo-feather wings and peach-pip eyes to the flagpole, and it was hoisted up instead of the flag. It caused a good commotion. Teachers got angry. Kids threw stuff at it. Pim never said he did it, but I know he did.

I'm one of the 11-percenters. But I don't pipe up about it. If I could shine on the sporting field, maybe I'd be up for a bit of boasting. Or if I had a band, like Kenny's, that would be something. If I had that Neil Armstrong grit, I'd just go in and ask Kenny if I could join.

I walk home with Digby. The frogs sound lazy like summer and fat and full of their croaking song, and dragonflies zip around as if in a mad tizz. The tall reeds have that secretive air, which means they are probably harboring snakes. Digby is looking out for water boatmen and mayflies. I'm not looking out for anything; I'm just looking. I've got my extra peanut-butter-and-honey sandwiches, as well as an apple, some roasted cashews and a blueberry muffin, all squirreled away for Marsh.

Digby says, "A snail can sleep for three years straight. Imagine that. You could go to sleep a kid and wake up a teenager. Or you could skip puberty and go straight to the pub!"

Puberty. I don't like that word. It's just icky. And slightly pushy.

"Let's skip puberty. Puberty sounds freaky," I say. Growing up without a destiny, without something to guide you out of yourself, makes me feel all at sea without a rudder.

"Yeah—you wake up and your legs are longer than they used to be, which is sort of similar to how it must be when a snail wakes up after three years," says Digby.

Digby seems to have been in the gangly stage since he could walk, but I don't mention this.

"What about girls?" I say.

"Girls?" Digby blinks blankly. Girls don't interest him, unless they are queen bees or praying mantises. "I don't know about girls," he says. "Though, get this, the female black widow spider's venom is deadlier than a rattlesnake's." Digby raises his brows and shoots me a deadly look, as if to say, *Watch out.* But he doesn't know anything about Marsh. And Marsh isn't venomous. She's fiery and strange, but not deadly. At least she doesn't seem deadly. I consider trying to tell Digby about her again, but I just can't imagine how he will take it. He may suspect I have a crush. And if he suggests that, I might blush or something, even if I'm not sure why I'm thinking a lot about Marsh.

I like the ways Digby is different from me. Our friendship is like a familiar room, something you can enter into, but Marsh feels like a doorway into a place I've never been. Which is why I'm going there by myself.

I say goodbye to Digby on the creek path. He is caught up examining algae. I tell him I have to keep going, as Mum wants me home early to look after Opal, which is a lie. I feel a little bad about it, as I haven't ever actually told Digby a lie before. Maybe this is a sign of puberty. I check my legs, but they feel just like they always have. They feel like mine.

Legs are pretty important, it occurs to me right then, and I just take them for granted. Mum is always going on about all the things we take for granted, like clean water and a house. When I had chicken pox, I was glad afterward for being free of chicken pox. Boy, I was glad—I was even glad just to be feeling so glad. Sometimes you have to have something taken away before you realize what it means to you, which is a shame, really. So maybe I should spend a day without legs so that I can be grateful for them the next day. . . .

My thoughts speed along because I am excited or nervous or possibly both. I swing by home. I take out my stash of food for Marsh and hide it at the front gate. Then I go inside, dump my schoolbag, rough up Opal's hair, say hi to Mum and tell her I'm going up the hill. I grab an apple and call for Black Betty. And then we are off, up the hill, sandwiches and all.

The tree house is quiet as we approach. I whistle to let Marsh know we are here. She comes to the side of the tree house and looks down at us. She is wearing a white hat. It's hard to tell, but I think I detect a smile, or just the tiniest sense of one.

"You've come back," she declares.

"Looks like it," I say.

She climbs down and pats Black Betty, talking to her tenderly. She is wearing a long, shabby white lace dress, which makes her look like a disheveled bride. When she finally remembers I am here too, she looks up and says, "Did you bring Nutella?"

"No. We didn't have any. I've got peanut-butter-and-honey sandwiches and a muffin. And some nuts."

"Okay."

Just *Okay*? How about *Thanks a lot, that's really nice of you*?

Marsh gives Black Betty another cuddle and then climbs back up the tree. I expect the meaning of this conversation is that she's allowing me to come onto her cloud platform and deliver her food. Marsh really needs to learn some manners.

I would have been happy with just a smile. I don't ask for much.

The Eyes of a Falcon

When I get up there, Marsh is sitting cross-legged in the corner. If there wasn't an impatient frown on her face, she would, in all her white, look almost mystical.

She waits silently for me to unload the food and then eats the muffin immediately, looking at me as if she is weighing something up. But she says nothing until she has finished every last crumb.

Then she lifts her hand and opens her mouth and sings a long, loud note. It rings like a golden bell. She finishes and nods at me as if it's my turn.

I'm sitting opposite her, and between us is her world of small things. I shuffle a little awkwardly. This is strange. I wonder if Marsh is just too weird and if trying to make friends with her is like trying to make friends with someone who isn't real.

"Marsh," I say, "I'm not sure what you want me to

do, but I can't just sing like that. In fact, I don't even want singing lessons. Could we . . . maybe . . . just talk?"

"About what?" She is reluctant, I can tell.

"Well, for one thing, about why you are so hungry. Don't your parents feed you? Where are your parents?"

She frowns and looks down. Her black hair falls across her face. Her thumbs dance around each other. But when she looks up at me, she leans forward, her eyes ablaze. "My dad says the best place to build a house is where a plum tree grows."

"Why?"

"So he can make *šljivovica.*"

"What's that?"

"*Šljivovica* is a drink. We're Serbian. Now I'll show you who we have here. I have sung them down from Khazar. Little ones, and Mumija. Look how she keeps me safe." Marsh has picked up the acorn again. She glances at me to see if I will go along, if I will enter her world. I try to signal willingness. I try to be open. At least she is not expecting me to sing.

Marsh stands up. The white dress catches the breeze like a sail on a ship. She moves to the stool, closes her eyes and places her hands on her knees. Then she leans back and her face tilts upward. Her shoulders twitch.

She begins to sing. Her eyes are closed, and it is as if she is singing to someone, singing of something very tender and sad. Her hand claps time on her thigh. She is swept away. I'm not sure where to look.

Then she stops. Her eyes open. She is looking at the small things. She picks up the tooth and places it with the circle of objects around the belt buckle. She points at the buckle.

"That's Nikolai. He is very distinguished. Whenever he chooses to speak, the others listen. Nikolai loves a pigeon, a white one, whose wing is injured. He cured her. He only has to call her and she will come. That's why they respect him. But Charles, here, has knowledge. He knows how things work. He knows what the laws are, and he knows which battles were won."

Charles is the tooth. Charles, along with the periwinkle shell, the bottle lid and the silver button, is apparently listening to Nikolai the belt buckle.

Marsh suddenly laughs. "Can you see them? You can't, can you? Mumija says you can't see them."

"What do you mean?"

"You need the eyes of a falcon. Falcons can see everything."

She laughs again. She looks so stern most of the time, but when she laughs, her face shines with tiny flickers of light. I like her best when she laughs.

"I don't know what you want me to see."

"Close your eyes and look with your soul."

I close my eyes. I hear the sounds that come off the hill: the cars thrumming on the distant highway, the birds chattering. How do I look with my soul?

Sunlight lands on my eyelids, and diamonds of light wobble there. Marsh's hand is on my arm. And then I hear her voice, that golden bell, loud and full. Her song climbs upward. It floods the dark pools behind my eyes. There is a swirl of color, as if the darkness will be torn open, and I am straining to see what is behind the dark.

But the song has gone down. The dark rolls over and over, and waves of laughter spread like the sea on the shore. It's Marsh.

I open my eyes. I see her. Wild like the ocean and as beautiful as the night.

Nine Grim Lions

"**W**ell, you wrecked it," I say. "I was just about to see something."

I'm not sure this is true, but I'm also not sure it isn't true. I say it mostly to disguise my sudden burst of admiration.

Marsh shrugs. "Either you see them or you don't. Now you don't, but soon you will."

"How do you know I will? How did you learn to see them?" I ask. At least if I know what I'm meant to see, it might help me see it. I know she won't tell me, just like she won't tell me her name. So I'm not going to ask her. But I can't work out whether the small things come to life for her or are just the symbols of something else she is "seeing" in her mind.

She tilts her head and closes her eyes. She leans back on her stool again. "I'll tell you their story. And then you might see them." She heaves a great sigh.

I sit patiently waiting for the story. I prefer listening to stories than being put to a seeing test.

"Okay," she says, waving her arm theatrically. "There was a time when the Plains of Khazar and the Mountain of Tara were all one country. It was a very beautiful country ruled over by a king and a queen."

"Like all fairy tales," I interrupt.

She raises her eyebrows, but ignores me. "But then the king had a new adviser, Charles, who convinced him that he should become more stately and authoritative and should stop wandering around the land eating and dancing with the people. The queen, Mumija"—Marsh picks up the acorn—"didn't agree, but Charles warned the king that his beautiful country would be invaded if he did not show some strength and form an army and create laws and punish those who didn't obey. The king was distressed. He felt he had no choice but to protect his land with an army and strict laws. The queen became unhappy with this and ran away. She hid on the Mountain of Tara, where the animals protected her, as they always had. The king fell into grief and drank too much *šljivovica* to escape his sadness. Since the king could not rule the land, Charles tried to take control, but there was fighting, as others wanted to take control as well."

"You mean there was a war?" I ask.

She frowns, as if my question has brought some grim

reality to the story. "The queen, Mumija, lives on the mountain, surrounded by her nine grim lions, and Badja-neck, who is a young girl, brings her bread to eat." Marsh points to the silver button. "People can hear the queen singing."

I am completely confused about whether this story is folklore, history, fairy tale or something Marsh has made up herself.

"Marsh, are the Plains of Khazar in Serbia?" I ask.

Marsh rolls her eyes. She seems perplexed and annoyed by my question. "The plains are up there. I've already told you. You can see them with your mind's eye, your falcon eye. Serbia is far away, overseas."

If you ask a straight question, it's because you want a straight answer, but I should have known not to expect that with Marsh. I persevere anyway. "Well, who is Niko-lai, the one who loves the white dove?" I ask.

"He lives there too," she says. "On the plains. He also threatens the king, because the king doesn't understand him. He isn't like the rest of the people. Nikolai lives in a hotel; he has no wife or children. He can see things that other people can't see. He sees the mysteries."

Marsh puts the acorn down and places her hands one on top of the other in her lap. Her thumbs begin their frenzied dance around each other again. "You know, Joey, once a story has been written, it's best to cross out

67

the beginning and the ending. Because that's where the lying happens."

She states this as if it's a piece of wisdom she is offering me and I should be grateful. She looks at me to see if I am impressed. I'm not easily impressed by things like this. My mum is a poet; she hands down pieces of wisdom all the time. But Marsh keeps going.

"It was a Russian who said that. His name was Chekhov. Mama always said it to me. So in this story"—she waves her hand over the theater of small players—"there is no beginning and no ending. Up there, on the Plains of Khazar, everything keeps going. The bears won't ever kill anyone. No one gets sick. No one dies."

There is something spooky about all this. The Plains of Khazar don't sound like the sort of place I would be keen to visit, especially since the lions are grim. Maybe I don't want to see all this stuff.

"A story has to have an ending," I say. I'm sick of Marsh calling all the shots. Already I am second in command here. There are things I know too, and I'm not going to stay quiet. I know stories have endings, even if they are lies. Most stories are lies from start to finish. They're just interesting lies.

Marsh is standing up. She shakes her head, grabs the acorn, curls her hand around it and presses it to her chest.

Her eyes close, her face tilts up and her song erupts

from her. I recognize it now. That song haunts her. It carries her away, winding up to the Mountain of Tara, the Plains of Khazar, the skies and the circling doves. Marsh has gone there. She has closed everything else out, including me.

I climb down the tree trunk and whistle for Black Betty. We walk away from the peppercorn tree and the eerie song.

Suddenly home seems such a normal place. I think of our kitchen, with Opal on a stool stirring pancake mixture, and Mum singing along to Neil Young, and Dad brewing coffee, and Black Betty in her basket nibbling at some itchy spot. The chicken scraps bucket, the notes on the fridge, the fruit bowl, the Weet-Bix box on top of the cupboard and the never-quite-cleared table with the bunch of wilting apricot roses that Opal picked. It's comfortably lived in, and that's what Marsh's world isn't. I don't know what it is, but I do know that something isn't right. It could just be my overactive sensitivities, but I have a feeling that Marsh needs help.

Two Worlds

"Where did you go?" demands Opal. She is running full pelt across the garden with a trowel in one hand.

"Where are you going?" I ask back.

She pulls herself to a stop. Her pink wings are shivering, her hands are dirty and her hair is sticking out. She seems to have landed midflight.

"Me and Bossy are making cakes. I'm getting dirt," she says.

Bossy is an ISA Brown chicken. I can see that further up the garden Bossy is in the wheelbarrow.

"Where were you?" Opal asks again. It's hard to distract Opal when she wants to find something out.

"I went up the hill." I try to leave it at that. Bossy has taken advantage of being left alone to escape from the wheelbarrow, which means she will run straight for the vegetable garden, and Opal will get hell from Mum when Bossy tractors up the new seedlings.

"What did you do there?"

"Bossy's out," I say, to give fair warning. But Opal shrugs. She can tell I've been up to something and she is prepared to risk the fallout from Bossy's escape to uncover it.

"Where were you?" she repeats.

"Top-secret information. Sorry, Ope."

Opal drops her trowel. "Tell me." She stomps. "I won't tell anyone."

"Cross your heart and hope to die?"

She crosses her heart in an instant and makes the oath.

"Okay, I went up the hill with a book and I read a story."

"Is that all?" Opal is appalled.

"Well, it was a strange story. It's about a girl who lives in a tree and never goes to school. Actually, she lives in two worlds, the world in the tree and then a world above the tree. She gets to that other world by singing. It's called the Plains of Khazar."

I figure that telling it as a story gets me out of telling the truth, while it also allows me to talk about what's on my mind. Or someone who is on my mind.

Opal grins in delight. "Why don't her parents make her go to school?"

I shrug. There are holes in the story, that's for sure. "The book doesn't talk about parents. Who wants to read a story about parents?"

"What's the other world like? Does it have a tin man?" Opal has watched *The Wizard of Oz* too many times.

"No. There is a man who mends the wings of a dove. And people with names in another language. Wars, of course. And a queen hiding on the top of a mountain with nine grim lions protecting her, and a little girl who brings her food. There are bears too."

"Real bears? Or pretend bears?"

That's the question I keep turning over in my mind. Are the Plains of Khazar real or not? There is no doubt that Marsh is seeing something. Can people really go to another place without moving? I suppose you can when you sleep.

"Dream bears," I say.

Opal ponders this a moment. She seems to like it. "Sounds like a cartoon!" she yells, running back to her wheelbarrow. To her it's all like a cartoon—dream bears, a tin man, a mud pie and somersaults.

I go and get my guitar. I sit on the front porch where Opal can't see me and won't bug me anymore. I like playing my guitar when I expect nothing from it. Sometimes I look for something—I want the guitar to sing me my song—but other times it's just like doodling. I can think over the top of it—it leads me to a sort of dream-think, a thinking that's loose and wandering—with half an ear on the notes and half an eye on the thoughts.

I'm thinking about Opal and how she is enthusiastic for anything and then drops it as if nothing matters too much. She bubbles over like water. And this is exactly how Marsh isn't.

Marsh is like an ocean wave, always coming forward. Whatever it is that matters to her really matters, and it gets in her heart and takes over. When she sings that song, the one that takes her away, she is wholly herself; she isn't trying to perform or to be someone I might like or the other kids might like. And she doesn't care about opinions, because she isn't even thinking; she is just alive to the very ends of her toes and fingers. And all of her is in the song. And the way she does that is beautiful in the way the ocean is beautiful. And when I hear her, it feels as if my little self comes out of hiding.

I am not sure what this is. All I know is that I am thinking about her a lot. And the thought of seeing her again sets my insides rollicking. It could just be it's because I don't know anyone else who could dream a world where nothing ends, where no one gets sick and maybe no one goes away, and wholly believe it. Or it could be that this is what a crush feels like.

15

A Speck of Air

Over breakfast I say, "Who knows about Serbia?"

Dad is trying to brush Opal's hair for school. Opal is making faces. Mum is eating muesli. "All I know is, when I was a kid, there was a war there," Dad says.

"What's Serbia?" Opal says.

"It's a country, in eastern Europe," says Mum.

"Did you put date balls in my lunch box again? I don't like them," Opal groans at Mum, who gets up to rinse her bowl. This seems to be the end of my conversation. I kind of hoped Dad might show some more interest, but maybe the morning is the wrong time to bring up important conversation topics.

I google Serbia instead, but even though I can see there was a sort of civil war, which must have been the reason Marsh's parents left, it doesn't really shed much light on

Marsh. But it might explain the war in her story of the plains.

I would like to invite Marsh to come to our house, but I don't know if she would. When I picture her sitting at the dinner table in her long white dress with her black hair and blazing eyes, it looks strange. If I picture Digby there, stooped over some spaghetti, it works. If I picture Kenny Lopez or any of the other guys there, it embarrasses me straightaway, not that I would ever invite them over. I'd be too afraid that they'd say no or, if they did come, that they'd be bored, that they wouldn't really want to hang around with me, since I don't play cricket or ride a skateboard. . . . And if they saw my guitar, then they would all know I fancy myself a guitar player.

But Marsh? What would she say? Who would she boss around in my house? What would she talk about?

Mum would try to talk to her about school or her friends or her home. Opal would ask her if she has a dog. Or if she's allowed to watch television, something Opal would be so envious of. Dad wouldn't know what to say—he's not a big talker.

What is Marsh's home like? By the way she ate up that muffin, I wonder if she gets enough to eat. Is her mum there? She only mentioned her mum once.

What if I could get Marsh to invite me to her house?

How could I do that? Best way is to be straight up and ask her, I guess. But if she won't even say her name, I don't like my chances.

Still, I can go in there and try. It's what you have to do. Be prepared to fail.

At school, there's a soccer game on at lunchtime. The guys are all playing, except for me and Digby. Digby is watching a trail of ants. So he isn't talking. I am sitting in the sun, half watching the guys, half wishing I was one of them, half glad to just be sitting there and not showing how bad I am at ball stuff. I know that's a lot of halves, but that's what it's like inside my mind. It doesn't add up neatly.

"Hey, what's the chance that this"—I point at the footy field as if it smells—"is not all there is?" I think out loud at Digby.

"High chance," says Digby. He peels a banana and examines the stringy bit, dangling it in the sun.

"Even this world here, of school." I continue thinking out loud. "All it amounts to is just one slab of grass with a concrete toilet block and a whole lot of classrooms swarming with kids. That's all. It's the tiniest of worlds. It's nothing, really. A speck on the planet's surface."

Digby looks at me as if this is so obvious that it is hardly worth pointing out. He elaborates anyway. "Well, when you think that Earth is just a tiny pale blue dot in the vastness of space, that makes school and everything in it too insignificant to even rate a blink of concern."

Digby blinks to show just how insignificant.

It's easy for him. He isn't the one wishing he could join in. It's me who wishes that. But sometimes I get free of it.

"Yeah, it's all just a moment in the long unwinding of a life," I say. I suddenly feel light, like a speck of air myself. The freewheeling piece of air that I become just keeps going. "Even being in the Battle of the Bands would mean nothing in the long run. Can you imagine Kurt Cobain"—heard of him? A very fine songwriter and cool misfit grunge-rock innovator who died young that I happen to admire—"talking about it, if he ever even won a Battle of the Bands competition when he was at school?"

Digby nods as if this is true too. I realize then that even Digby, my best friend, knows nothing about how much that would mean to me. If I can't be honest with him, what kind of a friend am I? A faker?

It's about time I come clean and just admit that I do want to be something and I am afraid of not being good enough, but before I even open my mouth, Pim Wilder sits down with us. He has never done that before. He must have sensed an interesting conversation.

"What's going on?" he says.

I'm half flabbergasted and half flattered and half alarmed. I know, three halves again. What do I tell him?

What I want to say is, *Well, Pim, you see how all those guys there are playing footy? Well, who cares about it, who even knows about it? Who will even know about it in ten years' time? Maybe one of them will get a silver trophy and put it on his mantelpiece, where no one will really notice it anyway, unless he points it out.*

Instead, I say, "You probably don't want to know." I've reverted to my timid self before I can even kick myself. What happened to being prepared to fail?

Pim shrugs and stands up. "Wouldn't have asked if I didn't want to know."

He walks off before I can try again.

I don't care.

I do care.

I don't care.

I do.

It's a shame that I didn't just say the truth, that I didn't just say what I was thinking. And it's disappointing that I didn't rise to the occasion, because, really, I'm in the mood for it. The mood for rising up.

Believing

After school, Mum is in the vegetable garden. I raid the pantry for food for Marsh and stuff it all in a shopping bag. Grapes, rice cakes, almonds, hummus, a couple of bread rolls and some cheese. I slip out before Mum comes back in. I leave a note: *Gone to Digby's. Won't be long.* Another little lie. I don't like writing it. I'm not sure how long I can keep Marsh a secret, but maybe I don't have to. But everything about her seems so hidden from the real world that I feel like I should keep her at a safe distance from my world. Maybe my real world would just clobber her make-believe one. At dinner last night, Dad asked me how my metal project was going. For a moment I forgot I'd told him that lie. I nearly blew it.

"Oh, we're finished with that project now," I stumbled.

"What was it about?" said Mum, pretending to be

interested. Mum drifts off when people start talking about cars, football or technology.

"We were acting stuff out about history, about how people made their weapons," I lied again.

"Did you shoot arrows?" said Opal, with her mouth full of apple crumble.

"Don't talk with your mouth full, Opal," said Mum. "Who were you with, Joey?" Mum was checking to see if I've made any new friends. I wish she wouldn't do that. There are some things, like not having loads of friends, that I don't need to be reminded about.

"It was just me and Digby."

"So you don't need a shield, then?" said Dad.

I almost grinned. I do need a shield with Marsh. But not that kind of shield. Just a shield of tough skin. Dad can't make that; only life makes that.

I take the food stash and head up the hill, as determined as any thin-skinned explorer can be. Even Black Betty seems to sense a certain determination in my stride. She runs ahead to clear the way.

What I like about the hill is how it gives perspective, how it gives a sense of the smallness of self in the largeness of the world. Back at school it's a different story. School belongs to the smart guys, the sporty guys and even the geeks. But the hill belongs to me. Or us. Me and Marsh. What we look out over is completely open, wild and as big as space. Nothing snags your eye down to the small, common goings-on, like what's going on in the schoolyard.

I feel larger with each step.

I call out before I get to the tree house. And when Marsh pops her head out, I give her a hearty wave. She disappears immediately.

I climb up. She is sitting in the corner, just like last time. She is wearing a long embroidered yellow shirtdress and sneakers this time. Her hair is plaited and wound around the top of her head like a wreath. I thrust the bag of food at her.

She shakes her head.

"Don't you want it?" I ask.

"First we have to sing."

"But I don't want to sing. I'm no good at it," I say. I plonk myself down in the opposite corner. I hate having to do things I'm no good at. Here I was, ready with supplies, a plan and a twinge of raw courage, and now I'm suddenly deflated.

"So? I don't care if you are no good at it. It's the deal."

"I don't need anything in return for the food, though." I open the bag and take out the grapes and the cheese, trying to tempt her. I know it won't work, but I do it anyway. Marsh won't back down. She sees the food and lifts her chin away from it.

"I have a song to teach you. First we will just sing the notes with an *ah* sound. I will sing a line and then you copy."

As she opens her mouth to start, I am shaking my head. How did I get myself into a tree house with a girl who is making me sing? How? I am about to be a complete failure. It's not that I don't like music. It's the exact opposite—I have so much awe for music that I don't want to crash my voice up against it. I know when things sound good and when they don't, which is why I never try to sing. I only sing in my head. I'd never sing out loud. I would ruin the music.

She is waiting.

"I don't sing. Sorry. That's the way it is," I say.

"You're just afraid," she says.

We lock eyes. It's as if we are banging up against each other.

"I'm not afraid," I say.

"Prove it, then."

We are in a fistfight, except it's words we are flinging back and forth. I remind myself that I don't have to prove anything to her. I'm not sure whether I'm angry or amused. And then, before I know what I feel, my mouth opens and I push out a long, loud note of pain right back at her.

She laughs. "Okay, you're not scared, but did you mean to sound like a cow?"

Because she is usually so serious, when Marsh laughs, it's like rain just fell on the desert, and because I want more rain to fall, so to speak, I throw away all my resistance and do it again. This time I try for some sort of human sound. It's not so bad. It's not good, but it's not so bad.

Marsh nods. She is neither impressed nor disappointed.

She sings the next line.

I roll my eyes.

She sings it again.

I can't win this one. But maybe winning isn't always the best move.

I shrug. I let out a sound.

She smiles and nods. I smile too. This feels good. I've had my private win. I've got us smiling at each other.

We go on like this for a while. Then she sings two lines and I copy. I stop caring how I sound. It isn't long before I know the tune, and then we sing it together. We *ah-la-laaa* it together. It doesn't sound bad. At least I don't completely wreck it.

I can't sing it like she can. She soars. I aim for the note and don't always land on it. But by now all my shame has been used up. I just try again. I even start feeling light-hearted.

Marsh looks at me, as if she can see me pumping my chest up. She takes the cheese and breaks a bit off. She opens the bag, pulls out a bread roll, tears it open, shoves the cheese in and takes a big bite. "I think you can do better than that," she says through her mouthful.

I just laugh. Let's face it, if Marsh had been pleased or encouraging or warm, it would have been a shock. But I don't need Marsh to say anything complimentary, because I'm glowing on the inside.

I look up at the wind telephone sitting up there on the tree trunk behind her. "You don't really hear people, do you?"

She is busy eating now. She is examining the contents of the bag, pulling out the nuts, sticking her finger in the hummus. (I forgot to bring a knife.) She looks at me and frowns for a moment. She chews, staring at me blankly.

"You know, Joey, your ability to hear things and see things depends on whether you believe you can. I believe, which means I hear. Do you want to try?"

She reaches up, grabs the phone receiver and passes it to me. I press it to my ear. I hear nothing. But I don't want to admit it. I consider faking a conversation, but of course she sees through me.

"Don't you have someone you want to talk to?" she says.

I shake my head. No one comes to mind.

She pouts. "Well, it's no good, then. The wind telephone is for talking to someone you want to talk to. You can say whatever you want to them, maybe things you can't say to anyone else. The wind carries it all."

Maybe I would like to speak to Pim Wilder. Maybe Kenny Lopez. Maybe I could ask him if I could join his band.

"Show me, then." I pass the receiver back to her.

She plonks it back on the hook. "I only talk in private," she declares, standing up. "Come on. I'll teach you something else."

It annoys me that Marsh assumes she has so much to teach me. One thing I could teach her is how to learn stuff from other kids. It's enough that she has taken command of the hill. It's enough that I had to back down and let her stay. Now she expects me to let her take charge. I change the subject, just like she does when she doesn't feel like answering.

"Were you born in Serbia?"

"No, here." She stomps her foot as if to indicate the spot.

"So are you Serbian or Australian?"

Marsh screws up her nose, as if this question has a bad smell to it. For a moment I expect she will ignore it, but she sighs. "Both. But sometimes it feels like I'm not really one or the other." She frowns, then drops to her knees and touches the yo-yo, which is still suspended above a jar lid of water. Then she brings the belt buckle to the water. When she looks back at me, she says, "Did you hear her? Eugenia?" Marsh touches the yo-yo again.

"No," I say. I have the feeling she is just showing off now. "Who is Eugenia?"

"She is an empress who ruled over Serbia. She wrote poems. And she became a nun."

"How has she become a yo-yo now?"

Marsh looks surprised that I would ask her this. "She is not a yo-yo. This is just the thing I use for her. It is about seeing with your mind's eye."

"What did she say to you?"

"I can't tell you what she said. Not everything is communicated in words. Sometimes it's just feelings."

I must look dumbfounded or disbelieving, because Marsh frowns at me. I can tell she thinks I'm some sort of blockhead who isn't capable of following her dream logic.

Before I can prove her wrong, she jumps up.

"I'm going to show you something," she says.

Something I might be able to see, I hope. I don't want to be taught anything, but I guess I don't mind looking at something. At least this is something I'm okay at. I'm okay at being open to whatever comes next.

The First Gift

Marsh takes me to the supermarket. This isn't what I was expecting. I thought she would take me somewhere a bit wild and secret, somewhere a bit hidden and unusual. I was not expecting the supermarket.

But in we go with no explanation. Marsh just smiles mysteriously.

I hope no one I know will see me here with a girl in a yellow dress embroidered with lilac-and-green flowers, a girl who looks like someone from the cover of one of my mum's old psychedelic records. Marsh doesn't appear to care who sees us. She seems almost unaware that there are other people in the supermarket, even in the world.

I know it will ruin the mystery, but I ask anyway. "Marsh, why are we here?"

"What is a special treat for you?" she says. "Ice cream? Doughnuts?"

It's hard to imagine she has money to spend on this kind of stuff.

I shrug.

"Golden Gaytimes, actually. But you can't buy them here, and even if you could, I haven't got any money."

She snorts. "I like doughnuts. In Serbia they are called *krofne*. And I like salted chocolate too."

I am still confused. We go to the chocolate section. We look at the flavors. I suggest cherry. Unsurprisingly, Marsh takes the salted one.

"Come on," she says. I think she is about to take me to the doughnuts, but she heads for the cash registers. She picks up a newspaper, turns to me and says, "For my dad."

Pim Wilder is in the queue, holding a can of dog food. Of all people to see, Pim is the best and the worst. He isn't the type to snigger, but he is the person I least want to shame myself in front of. He sees me. There is no avoiding him.

"Hiya, Joe," he says.

"Hi, Pim." I turn toward Marsh. How should I introduce her? I don't even know her real name. "This is Marsh," I say.

"Hi," says Pim.

"Hi," she says. She seems shy for once. Maybe because Pim is so relentlessly relaxed.

If he thinks she looks funny, he doesn't show it. He

just says, "I've got a friend with a hungry dog," and he holds up the can.

"We're here for chocolate," I explain, but as soon as I say it, I realize we haven't got any chocolate; we only have a newspaper. I glance at Marsh to check, in case she does happen to still be holding the chocolate and can make sense of my claim, but all she has is the newspaper wedged under one arm.

"What's the dog's name?" she asks. At least she turns the attention away.

"Maude," says Pim, smiling. Marsh has that dog tag with Maude's name on it. She doesn't flinch, though. If she realizes it, she doesn't let on.

"Good name," she declares. I catch myself hoping she won't show her wild-girl side, and then I feel ashamed for having been so small.

Pim nods. "Yeah, she's a cool dog." He smiles at Marsh. Maybe he likes her. It's his turn to go through the checkout. "See ya," he says.

"Bye," I say. It occurs to me then that being seen with Marsh actually isn't a bad thing. Maybe it's easier to care less about what other people might think. Maybe the real me is finally surfacing.

When it's our turn at the checkout, Marsh dips into her pocket and holds out some coins. It isn't enough. The woman at the register says, "You're short fifty cents."

Marsh shrugs. She says, "Okay, I'll leave it and come back later." She moves through. I follow her outside.

The supermarket must be a stop on the way to somewhere else, because so far Marsh hasn't shown me anything. But I keep quiet. Best to let the mystery unfold. Marsh is headed somewhere, and she is walking really fast for someone who isn't very tall.

"Hey, how old are you, Marsh?" I figure I might as well find out something about her.

"Same age as you," she says.

"How do you know that?"

"I just do. Anyway, who cares? I don't want to be any age."

Marsh has a way of acting as if she's different from everyone else. Everyone has a name and an age, but she acts as if she is above all that. Even though I might have a crush on Marsh, sometimes I'm not sure I like her. What I mean is, I'm drawn to her, but then she annoys me. My feelings move in zigzag.

Before I can stop myself, I've shot back a reply: "Yeah, and I never want to be so constantly superior."

She whips her face toward me as if stung, then turns away just as quickly. She says nothing. And neither do I.

I wonder what she is thinking and whether I went too far. Maybe she doesn't even realize she has such an attitude. Maybe not going to school means she doesn't have anyone to tell her when she is being annoying. If you keep biting, someone will eventually bite you back. If you keep acting as if you're better than everyone else, no one will want to be your friend.

We cross the road to the park. Marsh stops and lets out a sigh. She heads to the shade of one of the large elm trees. I'm not sure whether I should still be following her.

"Are you sulking, Marsh?"

"No. Just looking for somewhere to sit."

"Sorry I upset you."

"There is a saying in Serbia: You are not being honest if you burn your tongue on the soup and don't tell everyone else that the soup is hot. So don't say sorry for saying what you think, and I won't either."

I want to hear more Serbian sayings, but Marsh has already sat down at the base of the tree. "Look, I've got something for you."

She puts her hand down the top of her psychedelic dress and pulls out that block of salted chocolate, triumphant.

She is like a kid who has just drawn all over the walls and is excited about the drawing and doesn't realize the walls have been damaged.

"Marsh, you stole that!"

She shrugs. "It's just a supermarket."

I sit down and open the chocolate. I'm thinking hard. Stealing is stealing. "Have you done that before?" I ask.

"Most days," she says. She leans over and breaks off some chocolate.

"You must have a chocolate addiction."

She shakes her head. Her voice is quieter than usual. "No. The chocolate was for you. I get other stuff."

"Like what?"

She looks up at me. She's checking me out, as if she's working out if she can confide in me.

Eye to eye, we watch each other. I see she is afraid.

"Food," she says. "I steal food."

"And tools to build the platform with, right? You stole them, too, didn't you?"

"I have to," she says. Her eyes darken, as if to ward off any challenge.

I don't know what to say. I'm not even sure what to think. I stare up at the sky as a crow bursts out of the tree and swoops across the oval.

When I look back at Marsh, she shoves the chocolate into my hands and says, "I have to do it."

Maybe I looked too shocked. Probably she regretted telling me, but she says it like she means no further questions are permitted. So I shrug as if it doesn't matter anyway.

It is sort of nice of her to steal chocolate for me. But it's still stealing, and it makes me wonder if Marsh is homeless. I've asked her where she lives, but she just doesn't answer.

I have to follow her. It seems the only way to work out where she lives when she's not on the hill.

Come as You Are

When we get to the bottom of the hill, I tell Marsh I will bring her more food tomorrow. I walk off toward my place for a bit, and then I duck back and follow her. She is walking slowly now. She has a long twig in her hand, and she taps it on walls or the ground. I have a feeling she is singing to herself, because of the way she beats the stick. She stops often and looks at things too: birds, an apricot tree, a mother lifting a small child into a pusher. . . . Often she stops and looks in the windows of houses.

Finally, near the edge of town, she turns down a side street. The street is wide and the houses stand on moonscapes of bare gardens. If she turns around, she will see me for sure. But she doesn't, and I see the house she goes into. It's a small weatherboard house with overgrown grass out front and a wonky letter box. I creep closer to make sure I'll remember it. Then I go home. I might know where Marsh lives, but I'm still not sure what to do next.

The next day, I show up at the tree house with not only some cheese rolls but also my guitar. It's my next move. I figure the more I can show of myself, the more of her secrets Marsh might reveal too. At first I assume Marsh isn't there, as she doesn't look out when Black Betty and I approach.

I climb up and find Marsh lying on her back with her eyes closed. She puts a finger instantly to her lips.

"Lie down," she says. "I'm listening to the birds."

One thing I really like about Marsh is that she does strange stuff, but one thing I don't like about her is that she assumes I like her strange stuff. Even if I do, there is no need for her to be bossy.

But I lie down anyway. When I close my eyes, the world comes to me through my ears, like when I'm playing my guitar. Everything except the sound falls away. A train rumbles past. The tree creaks. And the air is a racket of birds—it's half conversation, half singing, some harsh calls, ticking, clicking and a lovely, melodic sort of trill every now and then. It makes me feel quite dreamy.

"Do you know which kind of bird makes which sound?" I ask.

"I know some. I think that one with the pretty song is a blue wren, maybe. It sounds like a musical alarm clock. Can you hear it?" Marsh doesn't wait for me to respond before she adds, "Mostly I just listen to bird conversations and feel part of the world."

"Did you know that trees communicate with each other too?" I say. My mum told me that. She says they talk to each other through roots and fungi.

I sit up. I'm about to tell her about the roots and fungi, but she changes the subject. "I see you brought your guitar. I've been waiting for that to happen."

"What do you mean? How did you even know I had a guitar?" As usual, Marsh seems to have mysterious ways of knowing things other kids don't know.

"Play me something," she says. "Don't be shy. I used to hear you on the hill."

"You heard me?" Had I known at the time someone was listening, I would have shrunk inside my skin, but now that the worst has happened without me knowing, it seems too late to be embarrassed. Instead, I'm a little aggrieved. "So you snoop too?" I say. "I think that makes us even."

She just laughs. "I couldn't help but hear it. Anyway, I enjoyed it. I didn't know anyone else came to the hill till I heard you playing your guitar. I did wonder why you didn't sing, though."

"So that's why you're trying to teach me to sing."

"Everyone should sing. My mum said it's good for your soul."

That's exactly the sort of thing my mum would say too.

"Your mum would probably get along well with my mum. Maybe we should introduce them."

"No," she says, already shaking her head. It's suddenly uncomfortable. "Play me something," she commands. Her voice comes out as if from the depths of some elsewhere she has momentarily gone to. I'm about to object, but I remember the aim was to coax her out of herself, not to resist commands.

I'm a bit hesitant at first. Usually there is a bedroom door or the wide space on the hill between me and another person. I'm a bit jumpy, but it's not long before I relax with it. I play her "Come as You Are" by Nirvana. I make a couple of mistakes, but Marsh likes it. She has relaxed again. I teach her the words. She sings and I play. Then she eats a cheese roll and tells me the latest from the Plains of Khazar. The queen was fed some bitter bread before she ran away to the Mountain of Tara. Probably Charles fed it to her. Badjaneck brings her bread now, and they both go to Eugenia for advice. Charles, who lives in a tall stone house, is the ruler of the plains since the king is still grieving the queen's disappearance and is always sleeping.

I notice that the more Marsh tells me, the more images come to my mind. For instance, I can see a woman sitting on the grassy top of a mountain, in the sun, surrounded by lions that are half dozing in the warmth. I can see Charles pacing up and down in a dark robe, brandishing some sort of implement—a stick, or a tool for measuring, maybe. In my vision of him, his face is thin and his nose crooked, whereas Badjaneck is wide-eyed, young and plump as a chicken. She's always walking up little pathways, carrying a basket. I don't admit this to Marsh. I'm afraid she will tell me I have got it all wrong. I feel like someone who is learning a new language and is shy about speaking it badly but busy storing away words to practice in private.

If I can see what she can see, if I can sing without fear of ridicule, if I can play guitar in front of her, then we are in the tree house as equals. But there's still a big difference between us.

Marsh has a secret life. Her home life. Whereas I want her to come to my home, she won't even talk about hers.

* * *

I tell Mum I have joined the chess club again and am staying back late at school. It's another lie, and all these lies are piling up on top of each other and becoming quite a burden. It seems even more important that I keep Marsh out of view now that I know she steals, but carrying the problem of Marsh inside me and worrying about what to do is hard. What if she ends up in jail? Maybe I should tell my parents that I know a girl who steals food and doesn't go to school. But I bet Marsh would never forgive me if I did.

By the time the weekend comes, I have decided to go to Marsh's house and find out the whole truth of what's going on. I'll have to get there early, before she goes to the tree house.

Mum catches me leaving. I try to creep past her while she is meditating in the living room, but she opens one eye. "So, honey, where are you sneaking off to so early on a Saturday?"

"Nowhere," I say instinctively. It's a stupid thing to say. She nods as if she heard that thought.

"Hmm. I'm beginning to suspect you've fallen in love."

"Mum!" I groan. I'm not the sort of kid who falls in love. A crush is one thing, but falling in love is another. Though maybe one step leads to another. The thought of this makes me squirm.

"Well?" She uncrosses her legs as if signaling that she is ready to wait, that an explanation is required.

"Well . . . I have a new friend, and I was going over for a visit." Yikes! Now I've let a little paw of the cat out of the bag.

Mum considers this. She smiles. She twirls her foot. "I'm glad. Are we going to meet this new friend soon?"

"Sure. But not today." I avoid confirming whether it is a he or a she—if I say *he,* it will be another lie, and if I say *she,* Mum will assume she was right about some sort of girlfriend business. Even if she is onto something, I'm not ready for her to know it. I'm not even ready for me to know it. Mum nods and folds her legs back up beneath her.

"Okay. Be home by lunchtime."

I run before she asks any more questions.

Outside it's hot already. The cicadas' dull, metallic song rises from the trees. There is no wind. I stick to the shady side of the street. I practice what I'll say. *Oh wow, Marsh? So this is where you live? How amazing. I was just door-knocking for the Salvos. . . .*

Another lie. I can't lie to Marsh as well as Mum and Digby. Actually, I don't like lying to anyone. It makes me feel all inside out.

Hi, Marsh. Sorry. I followed you. Because I was worried you didn't have a home and . . . well . . . I'm still worried.

I don't know. I don't even know why I'm going. Except that I don't want Marsh to get into big trouble. But maybe Marsh is already in trouble. Something isn't right. And I have to work it out. That's why I'm here. That's why I'm knocking on the door.

Ruzica

For a while there is no response. I begin to think no one is home. I press my ear to the door. I can hear a vague shuffling or creaking, but no one answers. I knock again, louder this time. Finally, the door handle is jiggled and the door is flung open.

It's not Marsh standing in the doorway. It's a man wearing a white singlet and tracksuit pants. His hair is dark and messy. His eyes are large. He seems startled to see both me and daylight. He rubs one eye and tugs at his beard.

"Yes?" he says. He leans his arm against the doorway and releases a stinky waft of underarm. I take a step back.

"I'm here to see Marsh."

He frowns. "Marsh? Wrong house, I think." He goes to shut the door. I forgot that Marsh isn't her real name, but I don't know her real name.

"I mean your daughter. I call her Marsh. We're friends."

His eyes focus on me.

"Ruzica? You are friends with Ruzica?" He has a heavy accent.

"Yes."

"I am glad. Welcome to our home." His face breaks into a smile. He ushers me down the hall into the kitchen.

"Sit down. You like some milk?"

He is already rummaging in the fridge. I notice it's empty, apart from a couple of bottles of beer, a half pad of Western Star butter and a half-finished bottle of tomato sauce. The kitchen is old-style, with a small table and two chairs beneath a window that looks onto a bedraggled back garden. There's a postcard of an ancient fortress overlooking the sea on the fridge, a framed needlework picture on the wall, a clock, yellow plastic salt and pepper shakers—the sort you might see in a takeaway joint—and not much else, apart from a stale smell.

"No thanks."

He roars with laughter. "Even better you don't want milk because we have none. Bah, milk is for babies and you are not a baby." He throws his palms up at the fridge and closes the door. But he doesn't seem in any hurry to get Marsh. Instead, he pulls up a chair next to me. He grins, rubs his hands through his hair.

"So, tell me. You met Ruzica at school?"

Ruzica? I can't seem to make that name fit her. "Yes." I lie to protect Marsh. When a lie is not for you, it's easier to say it.

"Good. Tell me, she is clever at school?"

"Well . . . we're not in the same class." I'm trying to avoid telling another lie.

"She doesn't tell you her name because the others teased her for having a foreign name. She is embarrassed to be Serbian at school, but she is proud to be Serbian too. It's hard being caught between one thing and another." His face opens like a sky with lingering clouds.

He suddenly leans closer to me and, as if something happy has occurred to him, smiles. "But you have heard her sing, yes?"

"Oh yes. She sings really well." I'm so pleased to say something truthful at last.

He nods. "And you? You make music?"

"Not really. Well, yes, but I'm not any good." I look down, not wanting to see disappointment in his face.

But he snaps his fingers and says, "Who says so? If you enjoy it, that's good enough, yes?"

His fingers tap the table. When I look up, he is gazing out the window, as if he is trying to see something. I shuffle on my chair. He turns back to me, seeming almost surprised to see me there.

"So," he says, "where is Ruzica, now? At school?"

I am confused. Or is he confused? "It's Saturday," I say.

"Saturday," he repeats. He stands up and goes to the fridge, scratching his head. "Saturday, and nothing to eat."

"There's no school on Saturday," I say.

"Of course. Forgive me. I am forgetful."

He rubs his face with his hands as if he is wiping away complications: food, school, Saturday. Then he slaps his hands on the table triumphantly.

"Ruzica has gone to get food. You stay, and Ruzica will make us some *burek*."

I have a feeling Marsh's dad is on his own kind of cloud platform. I have a feeling Marsh doesn't make *burek*, just like she doesn't go to school, just like she isn't really Marsh. Who is looking after who in this house? Her dad seems kind but distracted, or forgetful, as he says. And Marsh's mum? Where is she?

The front door opens. Marsh comes down the hall. I can tell it's her because she is singing. She bursts into the kitchen with a bag of pasta spirals and a half-eaten apple.

She stops and stares as if she has never seen me before.

Then she looks at me like she did when I first went to the tree house—with dagger eyes.

Before I can say anything, her dad stands up and opens his arms to her.

"So. What did I say? Here is Ruzica to make us some *burek*? Okay, my *maco*?"

Marsh looks at him with a sort of tired but forgiving love, and he kisses her heartily on each cheek. Then he opens his hand, gesturing toward me. "Look, my little tiger, your friend is here. Hey, you never told me your name?"

"It's Joey," I say.

He shakes my hand warmly. "Joey, welcome, welcome. Let's have a drink." He is standing at the fridge door again.

"Hey, Papa." Marsh shakes herself out of her shock at seeing me and pushes the fridge door shut. "I've got pasta."

"No *ćevapi*?" he says.

"Just pasta."

He sinks down on his chair again, deflated. He leans toward me and says, "You know, Ruzica's mother, Maja, cooked the best *ćevapi*, and wedding cabbage too. She would have made some for you."

He nods in agreement with himself and closes his eyes for a moment. Marsh watches him. She seems sad. It's the sadness I glimpsed the first time I saw her. Her dad stands up and puts his hand on her shoulder as if to comfort her. Something moves between them. It seems to pass through the weight of his hand on her shoulder. Then he turns and wanders out of the room.

Fault Lines

Marsh is frowning. "Why do I always find you in my house?" She throws the packet of pasta on the table and squats down to open a cupboard.

"I followed you."

"Why? You're a snoop. Why do I always find you in my house?" she asks again, and yanks out a saucepan, fills it with water and puts it on the stove.

I'm not even going to bother defending myself. "I followed you here because I was worried about you. Did you steal that pasta? Does your dad know you're stealing things?"

She turns back to the saucepan and lights the stove. "That's none of your business."

"Why is everything about you a secret? I don't even know who you are. You never told me your name. With me you are Marsh, but here you are Ruzica. Which one is you? Are you here or are you on the Plains of Khazar? Which world is your real one?"

"What do you care?" Marsh narrows her eyes.

"I don't want to be friends with someone who keeps everything secret," I say.

"He who seeks a friend without faults dies alone," she says, her voice like steel, as if preaching doom. I have the feeling it's another Serbian proverb.

She's got it wrong. I never said I wanted a friend without faults. I'm full of faults. In fact, my faults make me feel more at home with other people's faults. And none of this was what I planned to say. I was going to be caring and kind, but Marsh made it like a battle, as usual.

Maybe she can't help it.

Maybe she's just a fighter. Maybe we can't be friends. Maybe she's just too tough and I'm too sensitive.

Marsh glares at me. I glare back. Between us the air feels hard, too hard to get through.

I go down the hall, open the front door and leave. I walk along the street. I didn't plan this either. I shouldn't have got mad. It always makes things worse. Instead of helping Marsh, I probably just ended our friendship. But it's true what I said to her. You can't really be friends with someone you don't know. They don't have to be perfect.

You just make an unspoken deal: *I won't care about your faults and you won't care about mine. We'll just let them be there. Let's just be honest.*

Besides, there is so much I like about her. She can sing like an angel. She can imagine whole worlds. And she's original. She's interesting. She can draw people toward her.

I showed her who I was too. I sang to her in my not-good, not-bad voice.

Now I wonder why I even bothered. Why would I want a friend like her? I'll go home and I'll forget all about her. I speed up my pace just to give some oomph to my resolve. I'll call Digby. I'll see if he wants to go catch some tadpoles.

But I'm worried about Marsh, even if she doesn't want me to be. Her dad isn't looking after her, for one thing. It's as if some sort of Sleeping Beauty spell has been cast and neither of them can wake up to push past the thorns.

I slow down. I'm confused again. I wanted to help her but it didn't work. So what do I do now? Do I give up?

Around me, Saturday is unfolding. People are starting their weekend. You can almost hear the frenzy of plan making in the air. The footpath glints with hard, bright sun. A man in tracksuit pants is watering his pots, and a tabby cat curled up on a windowsill watches him. Cars whoosh by with people going to buy bread and eggs and the newspaper, going out for pancakes, going swimming before the crowds of kids take over the pool, going to golf before it gets hot, going to buy some tools or walk the dog or going to the market. Life is a whirlpool of other people's activities, swirling you toward something you hadn't decided to head for.

Life doesn't wait for you. It keeps going, keeps taking you with it.

I am heading for my hill. I don't want to hunt tadpoles. I don't want to fight with Marsh. I don't want to go home. I want to be free of everything, and then I want to listen to me.

How Songs Appear

The hill doesn't feel like it used to. Marsh has changed it. It's not my hill; it's hers as well. And since we are fighting, it has the grim look of a battlefield. I don't go near her tree house. But I can sense it, and I can sense her in it, even when she isn't there. The peppercorn tree stands there with a closed-up look. Maybe it is just that the day is hot and still and nothing moves. Even the birds have packed it in and gone home to rest, and that makes it desolate and empty. I go down to the pines, where it is shady, and I sit there awhile and try to have a long talk with myself. But talking with myself is like wandering around in a maze. I go past the same places over and over again, but I never come across the way out.

I'm worried, plain worried, about Marsh. But that's not all. I don't even know what I'm most worried about. Maybe it's that I keep failing. I failed with Marsh. I didn't hit the big time at school. I failed my dad by being a sporting no-hoper, and I'm hardly a guitar legend. Maybe I'm even failing at being me. Everything I try to do just sort of dives downward and crashes. My life isn't an arrow, shining and straight and strong and propelling me upward and onward; it's an old ball of string that is always knotting up.

When I finally go home, Mum seems to have forgotten she told me to be back by lunchtime. She is sitting on the edge of the trampoline, playing her ukulele. Opal is lying tummy-side down across the tree swing, idly pushing herself back and forth. Dad is up on the tree platform with a tin of oil and a paintbrush, oiling the wood. I try to slip inside unnoticed, but Mum sees me.

"Hi, Mouse. How is your new friend? Come here and tell me," she calls out.

Mouse. She still calls me Mouse. I never used to care, but right now I do. A mouse is a scared little creature that cats like to eat. I ignore Mum and go inside. I make myself a cheese sandwich. Opal comes screeching inside with the ukulele in her hand, letting the screen door bang shut.

"Did you see the girl in the tree?"

"That was just a story I was reading," I say, half surprised that lies just don't slip past Opal and half impressed too.

"Did you go to that place? Where the bears are?"

"I've stopped reading that story now."

I take a big bite of my sandwich and munch it gloomily just to show Opal that I'm not in the mood for talking. She screws up her nose for a moment, then rolls her eyes and snorts like a little pig. She runs outside.

I go to my bedroom, pick up my guitar and start singing one of the songs Mum always plays on her ukulele. Sometimes songs appear inside you, even when you don't summon them. I've never thought of singing Mum's songs until now. The sound of the song has a sort of backfence, kitchen-din familiarity, so it's something I almost don't notice, but once I start to sing it, it changes. Now I hear how the words mean something. I hear how the song carries the meaning along with it. The song takes me— I don't know where, but it's just great to be taken. I sing it out. Three chords and I'm away.

I'm somewhere I want to be.

22

Dark Horse

On Monday I get up early and put some bread, nuts and fruit in a plastic bag, and I go up the hill before school and tie it to a low branch. I don't climb up. I just don't feel like it.

And after school I hurry home. I want to play my guitar. I want to play songs and sing them out loud. I'm still worried about Marsh. I'm still thinking about her. I'm still thinking about the hill, the cloud platform, her disheveled dad, the Plains of Khazar and the runaway queen on the mountaintop. In fact, before I even intend to, I'm making up a little song. It goes like this:

I know this girl
She's a wild girl
Head in the sky
Won't tell you why

No, she won't tell
Heart in her hand
She's hiding herself
In a world of little things
Yeah, a world like that
A girl like that

It's not a very good song, but I like it. I walk around school the next day singing it to myself. I like the way it lives inside me, and anytime I like I can get it out and sing it.

During art class, which I like, even though I'm not very artistic, Digby, who is surprisingly good at drawing the bowl of pomegranates, leans over and whispers, "What are you singing?"

"Just a song."

"Yeah, but you keep singing it."

"It's my song, that's why."

"Your song?"

"Yeah."

"When did you start writing songs?"

"Yesterday."

"What happened?"

"Nothing. That was why I wanted to do something. So I made up a song."

Digby nods. Nothing really astonishes Digby, unless it's a small creature. Even still, he's okay. He lets people be who they are.

"That's good," he says.

I look over at his drawing. And then Max shoots a spitball of paper at my ear, which is a declaration of spitball war, which has to be done under the arty nose of Miss Tertle, which requires a lot of sly behavior, which keeps me from my song and the drawing.

For the rest of the day, I seem to be distracted from everything except my song. Each time I sing it, I change little bits, which gives me the sense that something is happening, or changing, or growing.

By Wednesday, I still haven't been up the tree.

It's not that I'm holding a grudge; I'm not the grudge type. It's more that I've got an energy inside me that's going full pelt and helter-skelter. It's as if my bones are pushing at something and something is pushing back at them. Maybe Marsh unleashed it. Maybe the songs did. Maybe just singing your heart out makes your heart stand up and ask to be heard.

Maybe. Because before I know it, it's lunchtime and I'm walking up to the music rehearsal room. I'm going to go straight in. I don't know what I'll say. I'll just show up.

"Hiya, Joey," says Kenny.

I'm inside. Kenny is adjusting his snare drum, whacking it every now and then. He doesn't look shocked to see me there—he looks just like he always looks.

"Hi," I say. "Are you practicing?" I try to sound casual. I'm afraid he might tell me to get out.

"We're about to. This is Clive." He nods at a guy on electric keyboards. Clive runs his fingers up the keys, butterflies over a few black notes and nods back at me.

So far, no problems. No one has told me to leave.

"What do you play?" Clive asks.

"Guitar," I say. Now I've done it. I've really done it.

Kenny raises an eyebrow. "You never said you played guitar."

He has every right to be suspicious. How do I explain? "Bedroom guitarist," I say.

Kenny laughs.

"Guitarists always start in the bedroom," Clive says.

"Yeah, I drove Mum and Dad mad drumming the table before I got a kit," says Kenny.

"I actually started on my mum's uke. It's small enough I could play it in the cupboard," I say.

They both grin.

It's going well. I'm in the band room. I'm talking guitar.

But then their real guitarist arrives. He looks quite the

part—shaggy red hair, white sneakers, black jeans, untanned skin and a guitar case in his hand. He holds out his other hand to me and says, "I'm Hamish."

We shake hands. He's relaxed and confident and sort of loose. He flops on a stool and sings while he unzips his guitar case. I feel a little buzzing joy, a secret little buzzing, swaggery joy. I decide it's best to leave on a high note, not to overstay my welcome.

"Have a good rehearsal," I say as I head out the door.

"Thanks." Kenny nods at me, but shows no sign of asking me to stay. Why would he, though? For all he knows, I'm not interested in their band anyway.

When I go home, I sing about it.

The next day my bones are still singing. That probably explains why I'm not only sitting with the guys but also talking with them. It happens like this. I sit down on a bench outside to eat my lunch, and Pim Wilder comes along and plonks himself next to me. We lament the healthy state of our lunches. Then Kenny Lopez arrives. Max runs up and takes a pretend mark by jumping up Kenny's back, and Raffie Langslow wanders over with a bag of chips, which he offers around. Mia and Sally follow Raffie, because he's the handsome one. Sally starts talking about the Battle of the Bands and how she and Mia are considering entering the competition. Last year at the school fete, they sang a song together. They weren't bad, but they weren't original either. I wonder if I should tell them, but I keep my mouth shut.

Then Harry Jay runs up with his ball and says, "Who wants a kick?"

My heart dives. Just when I was really feeling like a normal kid who was part of the gang, everything shifts to sports.

But no one answers. Max grabs the ball anyway. And Harry grabs it back. And then Sally says, "I will," and she laughs because everyone knows Harry Jay won't want to kick with a girl.

"When is the Battle of the Bands?" I pipe up, hoping to draw attention away from the proposed ball game. I don't even blush. I just say it.

Mia answers me. Mia speaks with a drawl. She has a long, thick, shiny ponytail, and her eyes seem to be always about to close. "Three weeks. March fifteenth. At the theater. Have *you* got a band?"

She says it as if I would be the most unlikely kid in the world to have a band, but she looks at me as if she is interested in what I'll say. In some ways it feels like I have suddenly sprung into existence, and I can't do anything except keep the momentum going.

"Sort of," I say. It's not so much a lie as a wishful imagining.

Kenny whistles. "You're in a band?"

Boy, oh boy. Now I've really done it. My mind spins. I open my mouth. "We haven't got a name yet. It's just a two-piece."

"Really. Huh. Well, if you need a drummer . . ." Kenny drums his thigh with his hands. "Who else is in it?" he says.

"Just a girl. Marsh. She's a singer."

"Is she the one you were with at the supermarket?" Pim says.

I nod. It's perfect. Pim Wilder is making my story seem true. Not that anyone would even think I was making it up. Why would they? They don't know what it's like to feel like a no one.

Harry, who has no interest in music, chucks the footy in the air and catches it behind him like a real pro. He says, "Come on, the bell will go soon. Who wants a kick?"

Raffie gives in and Sally follows. Mia stares at me once more, as if she's trying to adjust her idea of me so that it fits her idea of a guy in a band, and then she shrugs and wanders off too, and the gang disperses. But Max is still sitting with me after everyone else has gone.

"I never knew you had a band, Joey. Maybe you should call your band Dark Horse." He laughs at this and helps himself to some of my roasted almonds.

"Why Dark Horse?" I say.

"It's something my dad says. It means someone in a race who no one even knows anything about or expects to win but who wins anyway. Dad likes to think of himself as a dark horse." Max chuckles at this. Max's dad runs the bookshop, but he is also a part-time banjo player.

"We're not planning on winning," I say.

Do I tell Max the truth? We aren't even a band. Max would laugh. I start to feel my little performance tighten inside me, like something that is about to fling itself forward and reveal what it really is—just a dream I want to believe in.

A Plan and a Song

When I get home, Opal has my guitar and is trying to play it. I laugh at her.

"Here, give it to me. I'll show you some chords." I try to take it from her.

She swings it away from me. "No. I can do it," she says. "Listen."

She can't do it at all. For a small moment I even enjoy watching her not being able to do it, like she enjoys watching me not being able to do a somersault on the trampoline. But she doesn't care. She doesn't even seem to realize she can't do it.

I've soon had enough. I put my hands over my ears. "That sounds awful."

Opal glares at me. "It doesn't sound awful."

"Yes, it does, because you're not playing a chord. You're just strumming nothing."

She strums even louder. It's even more awful.

"Opal, can I have it now?" I shout.

"No!" she shouts back at me.

I frown at her. It's hard to fight with someone smaller than you. "Okay, you have it," I say, and I stomp into the kitchen to Mum.

Mum doesn't like being umpire. She looks at me with that look that says, *You should know better.*

"Joey, if you just let her show you something, then she will be done with it."

That's all she says. She is listening to something on the radio and I can tell that's all I will get. I am desperate to get my guitar back, so I'll try anything. But if it doesn't work, I'll resort to brute force.

I return to Opal.

"Opal, teach me your favorite song." I sit down, ready to be serenaded.

Opal smiles victoriously. She even looks coy. She strums quietly now, and carefully, and then she begins to sing softly too. She is making it up as she goes along, I can tell. The more I listen, the quieter she becomes. It's actually quite sweet in a tuneless way. Suddenly she stops. She thrusts the guitar at me. "There. Your turn," she says.

"Thanks," I say. "That was a great song."

Opal grins. Now she folds her arms across her chest. She reminds me of Marsh for a moment.

In fact, as I head off to my room to play my guitar in my imaginary band, something comes to me. If Marsh is like Opal, if she is always going to be too proud to accept help, then the way to help Marsh might be the exact opposite of how I've been trying. Maybe when I offer to help her, that makes it seem as if she needs help. And that makes her feel ashamed. And then she gets mad at the person who made her feel ashamed—me. So maybe I should treat her as if she doesn't need any help. In fact, I could go even further and act like it's me who needs help. If I ask her for help, or confess I've got some problems, confidence problems for a start, she may feel like she could at least stop hiding hers. I'll tell her how I have really got myself into a pickle by bragging about a band I don't have but secretly want. In fact, this plan could also help me not lose face at school.

I start to sing.

She's so closed up
I'm getting fed up
waiting
for her
To open the door
And let in the sun

*   *   *

By the following day, I have my plan. And a new song. And with both of these brimming in my heart, I go up the hill again. And the hill feels like it's all mine again. Which is not to say that it isn't also the snakes' and rabbits' and wood pigeons'. And Old Grey's and even Marsh's too. But I am in a very caring and sharing mood and I feel as if the hill is all of ours and that we are all a team on the hill. I get near the tree house and call out, "Hey, Marsh?"

At first there is no response. I can tell she is there, though. I just can.

She looks out long enough to throw something at me, then ducks down again and calls out, "Go away."

Whatever she threw missed me. I call back, "I'm not going away. I'm coming up."

I heave myself up the tree and into the tree house. Marsh is sitting there, in the middle of all the small things, wearing her blank face. She is dressed in her usual style. It occurs to me that she's wearing her mother's clothes, as they are always too big for her. This time it's a paisley dress with floaty sleeves, which hang in wafts around her thin arms. She raises a hand with her palm flat toward me. I think she is secretly glad I am there, even if she doesn't realize it. I feel like telling her to stop sulking, but that would get us off to a bad start. So instead, I ignore her performance and sit down.

"Marsh, I came to ask you to help me out," I say.

"So you're not here to snoop, then," she says.

I flinch a bit. That kind of hurt, but I'm feeling strong—I can take it. "Did you get the food I left you?" I ask, just to remind her that I had plenty of chances for snooping and I didn't take them.

Her gaze drops. As it should. She should be thanking me instead of accusing me.

She is quiet. I am too.

A breeze ruffles the branches around us. Shadows sway across the floor. The little things sit there, as if stopped in midconversation. In that moment, it's as if the real world is waiting like an audience for the little things to continue. The leaves and air and even the birds seem to have hushed, and the little things are there, bright and vivid in the moving shadows, as if they would burst themselves into life right in front of me. I look away from them, and there is Marsh, staring at me too. Something is drawing me in. Marsh is still watching me. They all are.

Marsh hands the acorn to me. "Here, you hold Mumija."

I hold the acorn, but I feel awkward, as if something is meant to happen. But nothing does, so I put it down.

Marsh leans toward me and whispers, "My mama wants to tell you something."

"Your mother?"

"Yes. Mama wants to thank you for the food you gave me."

"Marsh, where is your mum?"

Marsh picks up the acorn again and curls her hand around it.

I lean forward. "No, Marsh, not Mumija. Your real mum. Did she run away?"

Marsh stares at me, but she isn't seeing me. She stands up and takes the tiny basket down from the shelf, placing it on the floor. It is full of dried red rose petals and oak leaves. She puts the acorn in it, as if she is putting it in its bed. She does this tenderly. Her eyes move back and forth between me and the acorn. And then, gazing down at the acorn, she gently covers it with an oak leaf, just as you would pull a sheet over someone who has died.

Bitter Bread

"**Y**our mum died?" I exhale the words.

Marsh nods slowly.

I don't know what to say. I look down. I say, "I'm sorry."

For a moment the world turns a little darker and the sadness is so quiet you can't hear it. Birds dart from branch to branch, the wind whispers in the leaves and the shadows slip over both of us. Across the floor there are sharpeners and belt buckles and bottle lids—all ordinary objects again. But the acorn still lies beneath its leaf, as if it has died.

Marsh looks up. She is sitting there, cross-legged, soft, almost wilted. "When I was at school," she says, "the other kids thought my mum was strange because her English wasn't very good. She was shy. She was ashamed of how bad her English was, and so she tried not to talk. And her clothes were different. That's why I didn't want to be Ruzica. It seemed to make me strange like her."

It feels as if Marsh just became real in some way that she wasn't before. I want to tell her that the way she is different is exactly what I like about her, but it doesn't seem like the right time for compliments.

"So you did go to school once?"

"I went to the South School. But I was embarrassed. I didn't want anyone to come to our house because of my parents. I didn't want Mama to come to the school. I wouldn't even walk near her in the street." Marsh's hand moves to her neck and hangs on there.

"Did she mind?" I say.

"She laughed about it. At home we were close. When she died, I couldn't stop thinking about that, about how I was embarrassed. I was ashamed of myself. I would have done anything for her to turn up at school to pick me up then. I felt angry. I was angry at the school, at the kids in my class. I didn't want to be there anymore. I built the cloud platform to be closer to Mama. Mumija. She is up there now." Marsh nods at the sky.

"So it's your mum you talk to on the wind telephone? Mumija is your mother?"

"Yes. I tell her everything."

"Can you hear her? Can you really see her?"

"I can see her with my mind."

Marsh closes her eyes for a moment as if to test this out. Then she takes a sharp breath. "You know, I'm not afraid of much. But what I am afraid of is that one day I will close my eyes and she won't be there. I'll listen for her voice and it will be gone."

"Is that why you imagine the Plains of Khazar?"

Marsh looks away and shrugs.

"Who are the others?"

"Well, there is Charles, who is just like the principal at my old school." She pauses. "I never liked him, because he shouted at me for playing on the monkey bars without supervision. I already told you about Eugenia. Nikolai, well, you should learn something about Serbia. Have you heard of the inventor Tesla? Anyway, the rest you will work out yourself. You have your own imagination."

She raises her eyebrows as if this is in fact a question. Before I can assure her that I am well stocked as far as an imagination goes, she changes the subject.

"What did you want me to help you with?" she says. Her voice sounds like it's been lifted out of a well.

I want to say something, but nothing I can say is going to have the right kind of weight. All I know is my plan might have worked, but now I'm not sure quite how to carry what she has told me. All I can do is press on with the plan and hope that I'll work it out as I go along.

I lean back against the side of the tree house, bend my knees up and sigh.

"Okay," I say. "Here's the problem. I accidentally told

the guys at school that I had a band. With you in it. You and me. And there is a band competition coming up. And I said we were doing a song in it."

Marsh doesn't say anything.

"Could we do it? It's in three weeks. We could practice every day. What do you think?"

She gives a tiny smile. "Maybe."

"I've been making up songs." I can feel myself blushing before I've even finished saying it.

Now she really grins. She takes her hand off the acorn and leans back on her arms.

I grin too. I'm excited. For the first time I feel like I'm in the running for something. I don't mean to win; I just mean to participate. What a word. *Participate.* It's sort of blockish. There should be another word for it—like *flow,* or *whirl,* or *soar.* . . .

Before I whirl too far, I remember the plan. I lean forward. "But, Marsh, here's the deal. No stealing. I'll bring food. And no secrets."

She looks indignant. "I don't like rules."

Of course Marsh doesn't like rules. Obedient is not something Marsh is. I have to put it another way.

"What if you get to make rules too? And they won't be rules, just stuff we believe in."

Her mouth edges up into a sort of half smile, but her

eyes look black and defiant. She folds her arms and sits up straight. "I will be the lead singer of our band."

"Deal," I say, and I extend my hand to shake on it.

She shakes.

"I even have a band name. Just a suggestion," I say. "Do you want to hear it?"

She nods.

"Dark Horse. You know . . . it means the one not expected to win. It's meant to be funny." I don't confess that it was Max who thought of it.

She rolls her eyes. "I get it."

"Do you like it?" I ask.

She shrugs and pushes the yo-yo, which is dangling from a branch, the yo-yo she calls Eugenia after the empress who wrote poems.

"I don't care so much what it's called. I'm more interested in what we sing. Have you got a song?" Marsh is funny about names. It's as if she ripped up her own name and tore it into little pieces. I don't know why she doesn't want anyone to know she has a name, an age, a house or a family.

But having a song is something I'm funny about. I have a song, but I'm afraid for my song. I'm afraid it isn't good enough.

"Do you have one?" I say.

"Yes."

Of course she does. Marsh is fearless in that way. She wouldn't care if her song wasn't really the sort of song that kids listen to. She would just sing it because to her it's worth singing.

"It has to be something with easy chords," I say. I realize in that moment that Marsh could just take over and so I have to push my song forward or it won't even get a chance. But we can do two songs in the Battle of the Bands. We can do Marsh's song first.

"Listen. I'll sing it and then you can sing it too," she says.

She closes her eyes for a moment, as if to find the song. And before she has opened them again, the song pours out. Like honey. It's mournful, golden and thick. But how can I learn it? It's not even in English.

"What do you think?" she says.

"Can you translate it? I would have more of a chance of learning it if I understood the words."

She thinks about this. Her hand fiddles with the leaf. "I'll have to ask my dad," she says.

"Why? Can't you translate it? It's in Serbian, isn't it?"

Marsh sighs. Her head sways as if she is loosening it.

"Yes, it's a Serbian song. And it should be sung in Serbian. In English, it wouldn't make sense, and my dad would be sad. Mama missed Serbia a lot. She always talked about Serbia, about my grandparents there, and her grandmother Vera, who taught her to sing and to read. She missed her village. My parents only came here because of the war. Mama's grandfather used to shout out a poem to her on the phone. Mama would always repeat it to my father, especially when she got sick."

She stops, but I want her to go on.

"How long was she sick for?"

"Six months. But it's already a year since she died."

"What was the poem?" I ask.

Again she sighs. "I don't know if it will sound right in English."

"Give it a go," I say.

She draws herself up. She says the poem slowly, as if each sentence hurts her.

The sun of alien skies,
Will never warm you as our sun does;
Bitter shall be each bite of your bread there,
Where you are alone and there is no brother.

She sits still, waiting. I again don't know what to say.

"Bitter bread—it makes you sick," she says hastily, sweeping the floor with her hand. She looks down to hide her face.

I remember the story then. Mumija, hiding on the

hill, ate the bitter bread. The Plains of Khazar are a land where no one gets sick and no one dies. Marsh's story is all to do with her family. And her grandfather's poem sounds like a warning.

"Was your grandfather angry that your mother left Serbia?" I ask.

"He told her nightmares don't stop just because you change your bed. My parents were very young when they came here. My mother was only eighteen. My father feels it is his fault for bringing her. That's why he drinks sometimes and sleeps a lot. He is too sad to be awake. I was singing the song he sings to me. It's a Serbian lullaby. In English the words are funny. It's like this," she says, and sings it like a mournful plea.

My little girl is full of big wishes
My little girl is full of grand ideas
Papa, buy me a car, a bicycle and two oranges
Buy me a bear and a rabbit
Papa, buy me everything

It makes me sad. But before I can say anything, Marsh jumps up.

"I told you it makes no sense in English," she says.

25

Wild Girl

The next two weeks of my life are exactly how you would like the next two weeks of your life to be: sunny days with a friend, working on a project together up a peppercorn tree, all to the tune of a Serbian lullaby played on a cheap guitar.

I am brave. Marsh is eager. In fact, even though officially Marsh is the lead singer, the band—Dark Horse—feels like it's our band equally. We argue a lot, but it's not the sort of arguing that makes you mad; it's just the sort that it takes to make a song the best song it can be, especially when you are trying to make a Serbian lullaby into a rock song.

It only takes me a couple of days to put my song up for consideration. I sing it to Marsh:

I know this girl
She's a wild girl

Head in the sky
Won't tell you why
No, she won't tell
Heart in her hand
She's hiding herself
In a world of little things . . . Yeah, a world like that
    . . . A girl like that . . .

She cocks her head. "Is that about me?" she says.

"Yeah. Sort of. It started out that way." I'm headlong into bravery now.

She pauses. She scratches her head, wriggles her mouth. "Wild girl, huh?"

"Yep."

She makes her hands into claws and lets out a roar.

I roll my eyes.

She laughs. "It's funny you say that." She shakes her head and then snatches up the acorn. "Mama always called my dad the wild goatherd when he played the guitar. It was probably because sometimes he played like a wild person. When my father was a young boy, he left school and worked as a goatherd for four years. He spent most of his time wandering the mountainside with a flock of goats. And he probably sat under a tree and played his guitar while the goats grazed." She pauses and smiles to herself, as if amused by this image.

"Is that how he learned guitar?"

She shrugs. "I guess so. But let me tell you a story. It's a Serbian tale: 'The Goat's Ears of the Emperor Trojan.' It is about an emperor who had goat's ears." She cups her hands over her ears to demonstrate. "He would ask each barber who came to cut his hair whether they noticed anything strange, and if they mentioned the goat's ears, he had them killed. Eventually, he found one who pretended not to notice, so he made him the emperor's barber. But after some time the emperor's barber found it hard to keep his secret, so he dug a hole and whispered the secret into the hole. From the hole grew an elder tree, and from a branch of the elder tree a wooden flute was made. But the flute would only play 'The Emperor Has Goat's Ears.' When the news spread, the emperor was furious. He had the flute burned and another made from the same elder tree. But it played the same song."

"What happened to the barber?" I ask.

"Well, he lost his job, but his life was spared." Marsh is amused by this. She smiles at me. I can't tell if she is smiling because she thinks this story is funny or because she is just enjoying telling me a Serbian tale. I smile back. In fact, I do quite like being told a story, but really I'm smiling because she is smiling, and when she is smiling, my heart feels jumpy.

"Mama said that my father whispered his past of wild living with the goats into his music, and the music told that story, just like the wooden flute."

"So you are Wild Girl, daughter of a wild man."

She shrugs. "Maybe."

There is an awkward silence. My life feels very dull in comparison. Marsh fiddles with the acorn. I start plucking my guitar. I wish I was wild too.

"Anyway, I like your song," she says at last.

"Will you sing it?" I ask.

"Why not? Give me the words."

Just like that. She doesn't think twice. She sings it. She adds notes, or she warbles around on her way to the note, so the song gets more decorative, more bird, more sound, more frills, just more.

I say, "That's too much there."

And she pouts. She thinks. She sings it again. A little straighter. And so it goes.

In fact, it's all going so well that later I even agree when Mum asks me to invite Marsh for dinner.

"How about you invite your new friend for dinner?" she says.

"Her name is Ruzica," I say. Even if she will always be Marsh to me, I still think she should be proud to be Ruzica in the world. Now that I have given Mum a girl's name, she and Dad will have something to wonder about.

But if Mum does leap to conclusions about girlfriends and love, she doesn't show it.

"Ruzica? What a lovely name. Where is she from?" she asks.

"She was born here, but her parents are Serbian," I say. "She sings. We're starting a band together." I'm not ready to explain the whole story about her hanging out in a tree instead of going to school.

Now Mum is excited. She puts her book down. "What a great idea, Joey. I think that's wonderful."

"I'll see if she can come to dinner," I say. "But her mum has died, so if she comes, don't ask her questions about anything that might lead to that."

Mum looks completely shattered. Her hand goes to her heart. "Oh no."

Mum is tenderhearted. I suspect most poets are.

"Don't worry, Mum. She is okay. I'm just warning you so no one puts a foot in it. If she does come." I don't want Mum to get too excited. Everything with Marsh feels a bit fragile. Who knows, even though it's been going well lately, it might explode any minute.

I know Opal wants to meet Marsh because she suspects Marsh lives in a tree. Dad probably wants to meet Marsh too, but he wouldn't press the point.

* * *

I ask Marsh the next day. "My family wants to meet you. Do you want to come for dinner?"

Marsh pales. She leans backward. She doesn't say yes.

"You don't want to, do you?"

She shakes her head. Her large, dark eyes are fixed on me. She is like an animal, frozen and watching.

I'm not offended that she won't come, but it's disappointing. I want to tell her that my family is okay, and as I think it, I realize it's the first time I've ever stuck up for them. And into my heart they all land with an unexpected gush of warmth.

I smile. Marsh seems relieved. She leans forward to explain.

"When my parents came here, all they brought with them were tomato seeds, cigarettes and eight Coke bottles of *šljivovica*. And now . . . we've even lost the tomatoes. We've lost so much. My dad . . ."

Marsh looks away. I wish I hadn't asked her. Maybe if my mum had died and my dad was not really being a dad, then I wouldn't want to go sit around a dinner table with another family either.

I hesitate. I put the guitar on my knees.

"You know, Marsh, I'm not nearly as brave as you. You were right—I *was* scared to sing. That's why I never sang. I was scared of being a big, fat failure, to tell you the truth. But I reckon lately I've been borrowing a bit of courage from you, and I guess it doesn't feel fair if I can't lend you something too. I want to invite you in, that's all. If ever you want some place to land, you're welcome at mine."

Marsh sighs. She looks helpless. She puts both her hands over her mouth. Her eyes are full of feeling. But she can't seem to speak. Tears creep into her eyes. I have the feeling that one day she may well come in. If I had a little more courage, I would hug her.

Instead, I pick up the guitar again. I start singing. I sing just to sing it all to the surface. All the things we can't hold on to: life as it once was and isn't any longer, I guess.

26

The Guitar

The next day Marsh is excited and bursting with something. As soon as I arrive at the tree house, she makes me sit down where I usually sit to play my guitar. I notice the small things are all together in a crowd, as if waiting to watch me.

"I have a present for you," she says.

"Is it chocolate with a touch of salt?" I say, hoping she hasn't stolen it.

"No. Better than that. Close your eyes," she orders.

I close my eyes. It's always good to obey when there is a present coming your way. I hear her jump down to the ground and then climb back up again. Whatever it is, it must have been hidden on the other side of the tree trunk. Something large lands across my knees.

"Open," she says.

It's a guitar case.

Marsh is grinning from ear to ear. "Go on, look!" She's too excited to wait. She squats down, unlocks the clasps and throws open the lid. Inside is an old guitar, the color of pale honey. It has steel strings. I can tell it's a very fine guitar just by looking at it.

"Play it. It's beautiful. You'll see," Marsh says. She is already taking it out of the case.

"Hang on, Marsh. It's beautiful, but—"

"But what?" She is holding the guitar. It has the worn gold luster of antique furniture. And she seems to be shining too. But it just doesn't feel right. I know this is going to hurt, but I have to say it. "Marsh, where did it come from?"

Her eyes flare. She raises her chin and pulls the guitar toward her.

"It's a present for you," she says slowly, as if pressing the fact of it in.

I rub my face. There is no way around it. I have to ask again. "Where did you get it, Marsh? You couldn't have bought it."

She stares at me, with that same look she gave me the first time I saw her—as if I am worthless.

She almost throws the guitar back in the case, and then, without a word, she climbs out of the tree and runs down the hill.

I climb down after her, but then I remember the guitar.

You can't leave a guitar like that in a tree house. You could leave one like mine, though. No one would want to steal mine. I climb back up. I lock the clasps on the case as quickly as I can, but by the time I climb down again with the guitar, Marsh is out of sight.

I head toward her house. I have to sort this out.

If Marsh isn't there, I don't know what I'll do. I don't want to be walking around with stolen goods. I don't want Marsh to be hating me again. And I'm annoyed that she just ran off.

I walk fast. Everything feels urgent, as if the land that Marsh and I stood on together has just opened up like a gash and I don't know how to close it.

I arrive at the house and knock on the door with all that urgency. A let-me-in-even-if-you-don't-want-to knock. An I'm-coming-in-the-back-way-if-you-don't-open-the-front-way sort of a knock. Just as I prepare to head round the back, the door opens.

It's Marsh's dad. He is wearing a green shirt. He takes a moment to place me.

"I'm Joey, Mar— I mean Ruzica's friend. We met the other day," I say.

He shakes my hand warmly. "Ah, Joey. Yes. Come in."

I go inside. We stand in the hall. He smiles. I smile. He nods slowly. I am not sure what this means.

"Is she here?" I say.

He is shaking his head. "Come and sit down, Joey."

I don't want to sit down. I want to find Marsh, but I sit opposite him and put the guitar down. He nods at it and grins. Then he reaches over and picks up the case, undoing it. "Do you like it? It's a very fine guitar. An Alvarez. Handmade."

He begins to play it, bending his head to listen. "It's yours. Ruzica gave it to you, no?" He doesn't strum it; he plucks the strings, and the notes tumble out like running water. He doesn't even look at what he is doing. But then he stops playing and puts it down.

"I don't play anymore. It's going to waste here. You must play it. It is made to sing."

Now I feel terrible that I suspected Marsh. No wonder she was mad at me.

"But it's yours," I say.

I still can't take it, even if it isn't stolen. It doesn't feel right. I think of him playing it on the Serbian hills amid the goats and under the sky and it feels as if it should always belong to him.

He looks at me, waiting for more.

I struggle to explain. "I can't play it properly. Not like you can. If anyone is going to make it sing, you are."

Sing your secret into it, I feel like saying. *Sing your sadness in.*

He whispers to me, "You have time to learn. You are

young. You have a whole life, all ahead of you. It is your job now to make the songs of your life. My songs have grown old with me, old and sad and stale as bread. They are just memories now."

I am silent. I want to say songs never have to get stale. I want to say there are always new songs to sing. But what do I know?

But I have an idea.

"Give the guitar to Ruzica," I say. "Keep it in the family. She can learn it better than I can."

He laughs. "Ruzica has her instrument. Her voice. Her mama gave her that. She wants you to have the guitar. She told me you are making songs together."

"Yeah, we are," I say, and I notice how this makes my insides smile.

"That makes me happy," he says, and he slides the guitar across the table toward me. He doesn't seem to believe that I can't play it.

"I really can't. I never play in front of people," I say, and suddenly I'm sure the Battle of the Bands is the worst idea ever.

He frowns. "Don't be so small." He calls out, "Ruzica."

Marsh is home after all. So she must know I am here. She is hiding from me. Her father calls again. "Ruzica."

There is no sound. He grins at me complicitly and picks up the guitar. He begins to play it. Then he sings the lullaby, the one that Marsh sang to me in the tree house. He is smiling as he sings. He knows something.

Marsh appears. She glances at me for a second and then runs at him in a Marsh ball of fury.

"Why are you playing that?" she accuses. She stands in front of him as if she is trying to stop the song from escaping the space between them.

"Because Joey needs to learn. You give him a guitar, but he says he can't play it. You can't give fine shoes to a man who can't walk. So I need to show him. And you can help. Sing me your songs and I will show Joey how to play them, okay, my *maco*?"

Marsh looks at him in astonishment. Her arms fall to her sides.

"Papa? But you never play Mama's songs."

He looks down. His face is serious now. But he nods.

"No, but that has not helped me forget, and now I think it's time to have the courage to remember. They are your songs too, Ruzica. It's your job to take them out of the past and give them new life."

I wonder if I should leave. I stand up.

Marsh looks at me and then nods slowly. "Let's do it," she says.

Is she talking to me or to her dad? Or is she talking herself into it?

She looks at her dad. He is looking at her. His eyes are

so full of feeling I can't tell if it's happiness or sadness, or both at once. And then I hear Marsh's voice singing out and, beneath it, the song of that old guitar, the life of those old songs. And even if I'm scared, I know Marsh and I are going to take that song and perform it at the Battle of the Bands. And we'll make it new again.

27

The Battle of the Bands

When I show up for our next rehearsal, Marsh's dad is doused in aftershave and has dressed for the occasion in a red shirt and camel corduroys. He salutes me. With the same abruptness as yesterday, he thrusts the guitar toward me and takes mine. "You have to get used to your new guitar," he says as he leaves the room to get us all apple juice.

I am about to object, but Marsh gives me a stern look, so I shut up. She nods at the guitar, which I'm holding as if it is a star just dropped out of the sky. "It is his pleasure to give it to you, and now it should be your pleasure to receive it," she says.

"It's not that I'm not grateful; it's just I'm a beginner, and this guitar is for someone who can really play."

Marsh shrugs this off. So we leave it at that and head into the kitchen. There are three glasses of apple juice on the table, and Marsh's dad is checking the tuning on my guitar. He beams at us. "Come and let's start. You play me what you have so far. How long have we got?"

"Well, one week till the Battle of the Bands, and about an hour and a half before I have to be home," I say.

"We can practice every day after school?" he asks.

I look at Marsh to see if she agrees. But she is looking at me as if it's my call.

"I guess so," I say.

Marsh's dad gives us all he can. He adds melodic riffs to the songs, he adds notes to the chords, he tries to teach me harmonies, he laughs, he sings, he claps, he comes alive. Either he is breathing life back into that old guitar or that old guitar is singing the life back into him. We don't stop playing until it's time for me to leave.

I stroll home with my head full of notes and melodies. I go by the creek and hum to myself the whole way along it.

The next day, I go straight from school to Marsh's house. I notice there is a small vase of pink geraniums on the table. The kitchen seems brighter too.

"I cleaned the windows," Marsh says, without further explanation.

A few days later, a plate of almond biscuits is sitting on the table, which is now covered in a yellow floral tablecloth. I grin as I tune up. There is some sort of happiness in the kitchen that wasn't there before, and I know it's got something to do with the music that is filling it. It's like being inside a cocoon made of gold—me and Marsh and Marsh's dad and the music. And Marsh is light like the air. She grins and laughs for no reason, and her dad hums as he goes to the fridge for the apple juice.

I don't know when it happened, but I dropped all my shyness in front of Marsh's dad. He makes no judgment, good or bad, on anything. He simply says, "Try it like this," or "You could add this here," or "If you practice this scale, it will be easier to play that break there." When Marsh sings, he looks at her with the slightest of smiles, and his whole face changes, as if he is warming up from the inside out. I am watching this and it warms me too, but that warmth just seems to melt all those other feelings that I keep in cold storage and a little secret sadness seeps out before I know it. The truth is, I wish my dad could be proud of me. When her dad leaves the room, I can't help letting this out with Marsh.

"Your dad is really proud of you. I think it's making him happy."

Marsh smiles. She leans forward and whispers, "For such a long time I have been trying to make him happy again. For years it was Mama who was sad, sad about Serbia and being so far away, and he was always trying to cheer her up, and when she died, it was as if he had nothing left to do, no more reason to try and be cheerful. He was like a shadow, like someone who was hardly here at all. I felt like I wasn't enough without Mama. And nothing I did to try and make him happy worked. He hardly noticed me. So then I made my own world. But now that I am doing something for me, instead of for him, he is smiling and being himself again. It is as if he can finally see me again. Life is so contrary." She throws her hands in the air.

So what finally brought Marsh's dad back was the job of helping Marsh, helping to make her happy. He must like being useful, but instead of fixing things like my dad does, he tries to cheer people up.

I smile. My secret sadness can't be compared to what Marsh has gone through, but it strikes me that both of us have been quietly trying and failing to make our dads happy. . . . I've been letting the failure I feel around my dad color my world gray, and right now even I'm beginning to see all sorts of colors.

"My dad would prefer I was just some sporting hero," I say.

She screws up her nose and shakes her head. She gives me a little push.

"Maybe it's you who thinks you should be a sporting star. You should just be who you are instead."

Easy for Marsh to say: she's never been anything but herself.

* * *

At the end of our last rehearsal, we put down our guitars. We are all exhausted, but elated too. Marsh slumps on the table. Her dad nods at me and says, "Now, Joey, no more playing small. You have done well. You will make a fine musician one day. I am proud."

It's high praise, and for once, I can believe it. My whole being loosens to let it in, and it's as if something about the way I know myself changes. I know I should thank him, but if I try to do that, my voice might sound shaky, so I just nod too, and we leave it at that. I can see that Marsh is grinning at me and I'm not sure if she is amused by my little secret pride or happy for it. Either way, I feel embarrassed. She leans across the table and presses my nose with her finger.

"I'm happy," she says, laughing.

Sometimes I wonder if Marsh can see with her falcon eyes right inside. It's as if she knew exactly what I was feeling. I laugh, though. After all, it's the first time Marsh has ever touched me.

The next day is the big day. I'm nervous and excited, and I can't tell which is which, since both feelings buzz inside me. I meet Marsh outside the theater, which was once grand but now is quite dilapidated. Its shabby grandeur is just right, especially since Marsh is wearing her white dress—her mum's white dress—and she suits the care-worn majesty of the place perfectly.

"You look great," I say. She does. If she was my girl-friend, I would be proud to be with her. I'm proud anyway. I'm beaming.

She blushes. It gives me hope. "Are you nervous?" she asks.

"Sure am."

"Come on." She grabs my hand and we go in. If anyone saw us, and I hope they did, they would think we were going out. Now it's my turn to blush. Even if we are terrible onstage, at least we held hands on the way there.

There's a vaulted ceiling above us and the murmur of a crowd before us. Here we are, waiting where other performers have waited to walk onto that stage. It's just moments before we will be there too.

My insides are jumping around so much I feel almost fizzy. Me with the beautiful old guitar, Marsh with her angel voice. Me with my ordinariness, Marsh with her strangeness. Me in my plain blue jeans, Marsh in her weird white dress.

Me and Marsh. Marsh and me.

We are Dark Horse.

I look at her. She looks at me. We are smiling. We don't even have to speak. Marsh is perfect exactly as she is. A great original. She presses something into my hand. And then she lets go. I don't have to look at it to know what it is. I can feel it—Mumija.

Marsh whispers, "For good luck. Let's go."

I push the acorn in my pocket as we are walking onto the stage.

Marsh walks straight up to the microphone. She takes it in her hand. She turns back to look at me and waits. She is unruffled, composed. She is Marsh, queen of herself, of this moment. I nod. She nods back at me. We are ready.

Before us is a sea of faces. Out there is everyone who matters in my tiny world: Mum, Dad and Opal, Marsh's dad, Digby and Max, Pim Wilder and the guys. But all I can see is a crowd. It's like one big beast, shifting, anticipating, buzzing. I feel it fall quiet as I strum the first chord and Marsh's voice lifts over it.

We play my song first. It sounds like a real song. And I'm playing that guitar as if it's part of me. I listen to the steady, pounding guitar, the sizzling chords and Marsh's voice. I can hardly believe that it's my song. It's part of me, and it sounds great. It sounds big. It sounds real. I grin to myself.

I look out at the crowd. I glance down at the first row.

There's one person there, standing out. You can't miss him. It's Marsh's dad. He's so much larger than the kids around him, and he is wearing a red shirt and a red rose in his jacket pocket. He looks almost historical, like a figure from another time, and he wears all this as if he doesn't even notice it himself.

And now we play the Serbian lullaby. Marsh's voice is plaintive and strong. She is singing her Serbian song with the wild roar of her heart. It sounds different from any other song that has been played tonight. It stands out. I can hear the Plains of Khazar: I can hear Mumija's lonely song on the mountain, and the lament of the sad, lost king who stumbles around the plains, and the quick, quiet footsteps of Badjaneck, the young girl skipping up a mountain with her arms full of bread. Maybe what I hear is the sound of all that Marsh has lost, but I also hear what she has found.

I can see Marsh's dad standing there, swaying, proud, oblivious to everything but the music. His eyes are full of tears. He is shining like a rose in the dark, with everything that hurts and everything that loves.

When the song finishes, he takes the rose from his jacket and holds it out to Marsh. She bends down and takes it and the crowd applauds.

A Hundred Years

I would like to say we won the Battle of the Bands, but we didn't. We came in second.

Second!

To tell you the truth, I don't care. Second or third or nothing. I don't even care about the scores. I think Marsh and I even forgot there was a competition. All that mattered was that we played our songs and people heard them.

"Ruzica!" her dad says afterward, pointing to the rose he gave her. "*Ruzica* means 'little rose.'"

But to me, Marsh is like a swan. She is radiant and calm in her white dress, as if all this was meant to happen and she is just gliding on a lake while the water ripples around her.

Mum and Dad and Opal are all excited. Opal wants to hold my hand so she can be part of the glory. I let her just for a bit. Mum gives me a big hug. She gives Marsh one too and invites her over for dinner, of course.

She invites Marsh's dad too. And he says yes. He throws his hands in the air and says, "I will bring you some *šljivovica*." Dad shakes his hand and agrees, even though he probably has no idea what *šljivovica* is.

After that, we part ways, but as I'm walking away, I shove my hand in my pocket and find the acorn there. I pull it out and call to Marsh, "Hey, wait."

I break away from my family and run to her and hand her the acorn. She curls her hand around it and grins. And then, without hesitating, she puts her hands on my cheeks and kisses me quickly on the lips.

Then she turns away before I can even register it. She is running to catch up with her dad.

It wasn't a romantic kiss. But it was still a kiss, and I am swirling with happiness and stumbling home, head in the sky—the stars above the creek are shining just for me.

Dad brings me back down with one of those conversations that seem to happen in the dark by the creek after something big. "So, Joey, I can't tell you how proud I was to see you up there. I had no idea you could do that. But I knew you would do something—I just didn't know what it would be," he says.

"What do you mean, you knew I would do something?" I say.

"Well, I knew you would find your thing. Find what you love. Find something that's meaningful. To write a song and perform it like that, well, that gives a lot to everyone. Secretly, I always dreamed of being a musician, but I just didn't have it in me. I think it was what drew me to your mother, though. She's like you in that way. A real creative."

So all that time I thought Dad didn't like music, maybe he was just as intimidated by it as I am by football.

"But I think your sculptures are great, Dad."

"Oh," he says, "I'm no artist, really; I just like making things. You and your mother have got the poetry."

It's funny to think even Dad isn't confident about what he does. Maybe there are a whole lot of us who aren't, a whole lot of us creating stuff but keeping it in the garage, in our own sorts of garages, out of the light of the world. I don't dare look at my dad, as I was already feeling emotional and now this. Dad had faith in me all along. I keep staring down at my two shoes walking me home. Disbelieving and believing.

"I thought you wanted me to play footy," I say.

Dad seems surprised. "Really? Footy players always end up getting injured."

I let it sink in for a moment. Like a sunset.

We keep walking. Perhaps this is the best night of my life, so far.

But something is still gnawing at me.

"Dad?"

"Yeah?"

"You know, Marsh doesn't go to school. She hangs out in a tree house all day in a world in her head and she talks to her mum, who died."

Dad is silent for a while. "She's grieving," he says.

"Marsh steals food." I just blurt it out.

Dad frowns. He rubs his chin. "You know, sometimes things happen that are unbearable. Like someone you love dying. That sort of sadness is too much to carry, and so it carries you instead. Maybe Marsh and her dad need some help to bear this sadness. They need some friends, and that's one reason why what you two did today was so great. It brought us all together. We can make it a team effort."

I feel like hugging him. "I'm all for team efforts," I say. It's as if a river inside me starts to flow, because the worry about Marsh and her dad was the only thing stopping me from feeling completely wonderful.

"When are they coming for dinner?" says Dad, team member. "Maybe we can arrange for Marsh's dad to give you regular guitar lessons."

*   *   *

The next day I go back up the hill with Black Betty. The peppercorn looks lonely and serious. I imagine it is beckoning me. Before I know it, I am there. I am climbing up into the tree house, onto the cloud platform.

But it's empty. The little things are gone. The floor is bare.

There is only one thing left: the wind telephone. The whole place is like a strange phone booth. Not even the stool is there. The Plains of Khazar have been packed up. It's as if Marsh has disappeared.

She must have done this before the show, when she came and got the acorn.

I pick up the phone. I want to speak to the little things. They were what made the plains seem real. I try speaking to them as if they are there. I put the phone to my ear. "Hey, guys, the story hasn't come to an end," I say. "It's going on. . . ."

I imagine they are all there listening, even Mumija. I keep talking. "You would have been proud of Marsh, if you saw her at the Battle of the Bands. And her dad too. She sang your song. I think she sang it for you."

I'm talking to Marsh's mum. I didn't plan to, but I guess this is how it is with the wind telephone. I suddenly want to tell Marsh's mum everything. "I think you gave us good luck—"

"Hey, are you there?" Marsh yells out.

I quickly hang up. I lean out. She is standing down there with a spade, and Black Betty is at her side. "Come down. I need your help."

I'm all at once glad she needs my help and even relieved she is still telling me what to do. I practically jump down the ladder. And then I'm pleased to see she is still Marsh. She's got her khaki overalls on. She's got that wild look in her eyes and a plan simmering in her head, I can tell. And I'm willing to be part of it.

"What's cooking?" I say. "And where are the little things? It feels empty in there."

She leans on the spade. "Well, it's going to get cold soon. I had to take them home."

"Home?" I echo.

She smiles. "But I left the wind telephone there. We can still talk to anyone we want to."

I blush. Maybe she heard me talking. If she did, she doesn't mention it. But the way she looks at me is nice. She's just smiling hard at me. She is flinging that smile right up toward me, and I feel it land inside and wedge itself there, radiating beams of happiness through my whole body. I do have a crush. No doubt about it.

She lifts the shovel. "I want to dig a hole," she says,

and she pulls something out of her pocket and shows it to me. It's the acorn, Mumija.

It takes me a moment to make sense of it. "You're going to plant Mumija?"

"Yes, we are. Right here on top of our hill. We're going to tell our secrets to the hole. And when an oak tree grows, we'll cut a branch and use the wood to make a flute. And Mama will sing me her songs through it."

My heart swells. "Or we could make a guitar!"

"Yes," she says. "Both. There's a lot to sing."

"In a hundred years' time, though . . . I think oak trees take a while to grow."

"Don't always be so practical," she says. "Come on. Where will we dig?"

I guess it doesn't matter that it could take a hundred years for our tree to grow. What matters is that in that hole we put the secret parts of ourselves. You couldn't write a song if you didn't have something deep and raw and personal and only yours unfurling within you, wanting to come out, to say, *This is me.*

We dig that hole and I whisper my secrets and Marsh whispers hers, and then we put Mumija in the hole. The sky seems so big and bare and blue, and the sun is pouring all over the hill and catching sometimes in the golden leaves on the nectarines, and the world seems to glitter with possibility. And hope.

We sit by our newly planted acorn and sing the songs that Marsh's mum sang. We sing them, we howl them, we whisper them, while the sun slowly sinks below the distant horizon.

I have the feeling that because of our secrets the hill will now feel the rumble of a little change within its chalky old soil. And one day it will be a different hill, even if it takes a hundred years.

But before that, a lot of things will happen. Digby and I, for instance, will probably go dig up worms. Kenny Lopez might want to join our band. Marsh will go back to school. Opal will one day stop doing tricks on the trampoline. More songs will be written and more songs sung, and meanwhile Black Betty will probably grow too old to come with me up the hill. Maybe one day I'll get the courage to kiss Marsh back. And one day even further away, a kid will come and climb our oak tree, and maybe that kid might want to build a tree house in it. . . .

But for now the sky is dark and luminous and the sun is just a smear of golden pink on the horizon. There are a few large, black, shaggy silhouettes of gum trees and then the valley beneath, crammed with houses and dotted with their little glimmering lights.

The six-fifteen train comes charging down the track, and Marsh leaps up, flings her arms wide like wings and runs full pelt.

"Let's race it!" she yells.

I run after her. We both run as fast as we can, hurling ourselves down the dirt path. Before us, the darkening sky and the black trees and the valley of glowing houses are waiting.

And all of it feels like ours.

Acknowledgments

Many thanks to Jelena Dinic, a poet I met on an escalator, who allowed me to borrow from and plunder her memories of childhood in Serbia.

Also, thank you to Jane Pearson, my editor, and to Text Publishing.